PRAISE FOR *Fi*

"Filthy Rich is a sweet, funny meringue."

—*New York Times* Style section

"A delightful first novel . . . as timely as can be."

—*Tampa Tribune*

"Devastatingly funny."

—*Newark Star Ledger*

"Filthy Rich is a page-turner of a novel, and a guilty pleasure."

—Pasadena, California, *Star News*

"Filthy Rich is (a) funny, (b) really funny, (c) very funny, (d) all of the above. You don't have to poll the audience to know that the final answer is letter d."

—Joel Siegel, *Good Morning America*

"Did Dorothy Samuels write this book yesterday? This is the most up-to-the-minute reflection on fame in America I have read, and it's funny, too."

—Lisa Birnbach, author of *The Preppie Handbook* and contributor to *The Early Show*

Filthy Rich

A NOVEL

....

DOROTHY SAMUELS

....

AVON BOOKS
An Imprint of HarperCollinsPublishers

A hardcover edition of this book was published by William Morrow, an imprint of HarperCollins Publishers, in 2001.

First paperback edition published 2002.

Designed by Victoria Hartman

The Library of Congress has cataloged the hardcover edition as follows:

Samuels, Dorothy J.
    Filthy rich : a novel / by Dorothy J. Samuels.—1st ed.
        p. cm.
    ISBN 0-06-621016-X
        1. Quiz shows—Fiction.   2. Rich people—Fiction.   3. Television personalities—Fiction.   I. Title.
PS3619.A26 F55   2001
813'.6—dc21

2001030044

ISBN 0-06-008638-6 (pbk.)

02   03   04   05   06   RRD   10   9   8   7   6   5   4   3

For my husband, Peter,
whose supportive prodding kept me going.
And for our amazing offspring,
Jenny, Tom, and my indispensable
collaborator on this project, Laurah.
Together, anything is possible.

✦

Which legendary show of the 1955–56 television season ended the remarkable three-year reign of *I Love Lucy* as number one in the Nielsen ratings?

a. *The Ed Sullivan Show*
b. *The Honeymooners,* starring Jackie Gleason
c. *Gunsmoke*
d. *The $64,000 Question*

See correct answer on back. . . .

Filthy Rich

ne

✦

It's funny how a single dumb decision made in an unthinking moment of weakness can change the entire course of a person's life.

At thirty-four, I suppose that shouldn't come as any great revelation, especially as life's incredible serendipity is a central theme of much of the world's great literature, some of which I've actually read. It also happens to be a major subtext of the popular TV shows I watched obsessively while growing up, and whose humor and moral lessons still inform my general outlook and thinking—a jam-packed cultural cornucopia of after-school reruns and contemporary evening hits that included such indisputable classics as *Green Acres, Bewitched, Happy Days, Three's Company, The Facts of Life,* that trusty evergreen *I Love Lucy,* and my abiding personal Bible, *The Brady Bunch.*

Yet nothing in the seminal works of either Dostoyevsky or Eva Gabor prepared me—Marcy Lee Mallowitz—for the amazing, if sometimes traumatic, life-transforming rollercoaster ride I unknowingly embarked upon two months ago, when, against my better judgment, I agreed to be my boyfriend's Lifeline.

What is a Lifeline?

In the event you've been living in a cave, or floating on a raft somewhere in the North Atlantic as part of a farsighted scientific experiment testing man's ability to thrive once denied new episodes of *Friends*, I suppose I should explain.

A Lifeline is one of the clever wrinkles the producers of *So You Want to Be Filthy Rich!* built into the rules to add a touch of drama to the TV game show, and make it easier to give away the network's money. In other words, it's a gimmick for boosting the ratings, which—for reasons that continue to baffle me—have been stratospheric from the program's inauspicious start a year ago as a summer replacement. Who knew it would become a national phenomenon? A national addiction, really.

But it works. As many as five times a week—or even more frequently if the network's programmers are feeling desperate—zillions of Americans plant their greedy bodies in front of the tube to watch contestants perched precariously on a "hot seat" mounted atop a box of $100 bills field quirky questions for increasing amounts of money.

These questions seem to puddle-jump in no particular pattern from hard to easy, and cover an amazing span of useless, or nearly useless, information—everything from history, geography, and current events to physics and pop culture. The value of the questions keeps escalating, until finally the lucky player is going for the full $1.75 million—an amount calibrated so the show can honestly claim the winner remains a millionaire even after paying taxes. Answer correctly, and it's Easy Street. Answer incorrectly, and the take is a measly seventy-five grand, fake expressions of sympathy from relatives and former friends, and a future of excruciating second-guessing.

This action all takes place inside a circular klieg-lit arena—a knockoff of the set used in the original British version and re-created now in some seventy other countries. Given the demise of the Empire, and Princess Di's tragic death a few years back, I'd wager it's currently Britain's most successful export.

The show is broadcast live from the same New York City studio where Nixon and Kennedy met for one of their famous debates in 1960. The debate is mainly remembered for Nixon's bad sweating problem, which many say cost him the election, and I'm sure some wiseass Ph.D. candidate in history is already preparing a thesis comparing and contrasting Nixon's perspiration on that historic occasion with the flood that surely would have emanated from the forehead of the disgraced former president had he instead been going for the $1.75 million from the *Filthy Rich!* hot seat.

Under the rules, a stumped contestant is allowed to consult a friend or loved one identified in advance for help in answering a question. This person is the Lifeline.

When all goes well, and the designated Lifeline provides the right answer, the moment becomes a sickeningly giddy bonding experience for the contestant and the helper. When things go awry, however, and the Lifeline turns out to be just as clueless as the contestant, the worst family dynamics can kick in, only to be played out on live national TV to great audience acclaim.

At least, that's what happened to me.

"The Big Brush-Off," as some sage at *TV Guide* dubbed it in a callously accurate cover story, occurred at precisely 9:21 P.M. Eastern Standard Time (8:21 Central), just before the final commercial break of a Tuesday-night episode. During sweeps week no less. If you're a *Filthy Rich!* fan (and who isn't?), you probably remember the show. It's considered a classic.

My almost fiancé—Neil Postit (pronounced "post it," just like the yellow sticky notepads, as the program's nattily attired master of ceremonies, the genial Kingman Fenimore, matter-of-factly observed)—was on the hot seat. Somehow Mr. 3M, Neil, had made it to the $500,000 mark—astounding guesswork, when you think about it, for a thirty-six-year-old orthodontist for adults who never seemed to read much, except about the latest advances in braces. That meant he had just one more question to answer before either pocketing the whole $1.75 mil and joining the *Filthy Rich!* pantheon, or bidding an abrupt adieu to a singular chance for fame and riches.

"So," Kingman Fenimore said to Neil, "you've got

$500,000. Do you want to stop now and take it home, or are you ready to risk it all and go for the full $1.75 million?"

The large gap between the two top prizes is a perverse strategic ploy to bring out contestants' avarice and make it almost irresistible for them to keep on playing notwithstanding the considerable downside risk.

Naturally Neil, the greedy bum, fell for it. He just couldn't leave well enough alone.

"You bet, Kingman," Neil said, displaying more zest than I'd ever seen him exhibit at home. *Ever.* "Let's go for it."

"Good luck, Mr. Post-it," the host replied. "We're all hoping you can make this one *stick*. Get it? *Stick. Post-it notes.* I'm trying to make a little joke here, audience. You think it's easy being up here?"

Neil didn't crack a smile. He was tense, and besides, he hates jokes about his last name. If it didn't mean having to scuttle the lavishly framed dental school diplomas displayed prominently in his office, I'm sure he'd happily drop the last two letters and make it plain Post, an insight that may account for Neil's oft-expressed enthusiasm for Post Grape-Nuts, his favorite cereal.

"Sorry, Neil, I couldn't resist that," said Kingman. "I should save the bad jokes for my morning show." He was referring, of course, to *Gabbing! With Kingman and Tracy Ellen,* the ridiculously popular hour-long talk show he'd been doing weekdays on the network for years. "So back to business! For $1.75 million, let's play *So You Want to Be Filthy Rich!*"

Suddenly, the spotlights were flying all over the place, normal audience noises were replaced by the prerecorded sound of a pounding heartbeat, and the whole studio took on the feel of one of those old low-tech pressure cookers. A close-up shot showed sweat beads beginning to form on Neil's forehead and upper lip à la the aforementioned Mr. Nixon. The effect was to mar the boyish good looks I found so appealing—not least, I'm sure, because Neil's thick brown hair, clear blue eyes, and broad, slightly bemused grin conjured up fond memories of Ted Bessell, the amiable and underrated actor who played the tweedy boyfriend on both *That Girl* and *The Mary Tyler Moore Show*, TV's breakthrough odes to single career women, and two of my favorite sitcoms ever.

Right across from Neil, meanwhile, sitting behind his bulky game console and all decked out in his patented rich person's uniform of dark silk shirt and matching tie, Kingman, TV's reigning sixty-two-year-old wonder boy, was looking as cool as a cuke. And why not? Thanks to this gig and his live morning talkfest with Tracy Ellen, he was already a millionaire a gazillion times over, and nothing was going to change that, not even Neil coming up with the wrong answer and blowing his Big Chance.

I was sitting in the front of the audience with my mom, Francine Mallowitz, the still spry and faintly glamorous, if ever-so-slightly stooped, former second runner-up in a long-ago Miss Coney Island contest. I stayed busy cheering Neil on and nervously basking in my appointed double role of almost fiancée and Lifeline-in-Waiting. During particularly tense moments in Neil's hot-seat tenure, the camera would cut to a shot of me anxiously observing from the sidelines. On two occasions, Kingman paused the proceedings to ask how I was holding up. "Fine," I said, lying.

It's not just that I was nervous for Neil and what this whole experience might mean for our three-year-old relationship. I was feeling self-conscious. The current consensus of opinion seems to be I looked terrific. But catching a quick glimpse of myself in one of the studio monitors, I thought I looked pale, bloated, and, if you must be cruel, downright frumpy—in all, an unattractive facsimile of the fit five-five poster girl for glowing skin and minimal makeup that is mostly my positive self-image on days I don't have my period. I imagined millions of people reclining at home in their La-Z-Boys, wondering aloud what Neil saw in this auburn-haired blah. I made a mental note to blow up the trendy SoHo salon where my suave Italian stylist, the renowned Giovanni, personal blow-dryer to stars like Madonna, assured me between taking emergency cell phone calls from celebrity clients that a shoulder-length cut with multiple textured layers would bring out my recessive cheekbones. Liar.

"Members of the studio audience, we need total quiet please," said Kingman with a solemnity in keeping with the size of the cash prize riding on the next answer, and the show's pretension to be something more than just an ordinary game show. In just a couple of minutes, the world would find out whether Neil Postit, D.D.S., would succeed in his personal quest to wrest $1.75 million from the network. But the really fun part, as the show's canny producers well understand, the part that keeps viewers returning night after night, is the overwhelming communal sense of anticipation beforehand.

After an artful dramatic pause, Kingman continued.

"And now the question: For $1.75 million, Neil, which much-beloved hit 1970s television show, dismissed upon its debut as 'the worst schlock on television' by *The New York Times*, boasted regular appearances by the actress Teri Garr?"

These were the choices:

a. *The Dean Martin Show*
b. *Donny and Marie*
c. *The Sonny and Cher Comedy Hour*
d. *Hee Haw*

Neil had that deer-caught-in-the-headlights look. Sweaty and scared, he was morphing from Nixon into the Albert Brooks character in *Broadcast News*.

"I suppose 'worst schlock on television' isn't much of a help," Kingman said jovially, doing his best to revive his melting guest. "Some critics—I won't say who—said that about this show when we began. Can you imagine that, Neil?"

When Neil failed to respond either with a smile or nervous banter, Kingman tried a different tack.

"Of course, you know Teri Garr," he said. "She starred in some very good films years ago. *Tootsie* with Dustin Hoffman, Spielberg's *Close Encounters, Mr. Mom* with Michael Keaton, Mel Brooks's *Young Frankenstein.* You sometimes see her now in commercials for that lite music station."

The camera was in tight now on Neil's face. He twitched. He squirmed. Then, saying he was "clueless," he asked Kingman to remove two of the wrong answers—the other help option he still had left.

Now there were just two answers to choose from:

> b. *Donny and Marie*
> c. *The Sonny and Cher Comedy Hour*

"I'm really flummoxed, Kingman," Neil said, his game-show gusto suddenly spent. "I don't know anything about old TV. I'm going to have to use my Lifeline and call on my girlfriend. This is really up her alley."

"Okay," said Kingman. "No need for AT&T to place a phone call this time. She's right here in the audience."

As the host spoke, I felt my mother stab an elbow into my ribs, her subtle way of getting my attention. "Stop biting your lip," she whispered urgently in my ear. "And don't keep looking down. I want to see your gorgeous smile."

By now, the camera and lights had found me, and having somehow managed to stand without much noticeable wobbling, I was trying, not too successfully, to execute my mother's final order, and smile.

"We met her briefly earlier," said Kingman. "Her name is Marcy Lee Mallowitz, she's in her early thirties, lives in

Manhattan, and her profession, it says here, is 'Personal Life Coach.' Marcy what does that mean, Personal Life Coach?"

I knew the inquiry might be coming, and I had an answer memorized. "It means people talk to me about their problems, and I help them identify and implement positive strategies to solve them," I said.

"Sort of a cross between a psychic and a psychiatrist," responded Kingman with his bemused trademark chuckle. "Personal Life Coach. Sounds good to me. I think I could use a Life Coach. But that's another matter. Right now, Neil's the one who needs your help. Let's see if you can coach him to a nearly two-million-dollar payday. Neil, you have thirty seconds."

"What about it, Marcy?" Neil piped up. "Should I choose *Donny and Marie* or *The Sonny and Cher Comedy Hour?*"

"I'm only guessing, Neil. I've never seen either show. But I know Donny and Marie have been doing a new daytime show. Haven't seen that, either, come to think of it. It may have been canceled. I remember someone telling me that. Give me a second here."

I closed my eyes and scrunched up my face in concentration. Nothing came. The annoying heartbeat sound in the background was jamming up my circuits. Attempting to stay calm, I reflexively reached with my right hand for something to hold on to, and ended up grabbing a fistful of hair near the roots and tugging hard on it. If I pull out a big enough clump, I thought wishfully, maybe they'll stop the game.

"Marcy, there's no time," said Neil.

My eyes reopened, but I couldn't seem to unfurl the fingers gripping my hair. It was as if they were permanently affixed. I was concentrating hard. But it wasn't helping.

"Let's see," I said, endeavoring to rise above the steady pain emanating from one side of my scalp. "I know Donny and Marie are from a really big Mormon family. They sang, and dressed in hideous costumes. That's no help. So did Sonny and Cher. Except they weren't Mormons. And they didn't have a big family. Only Chastity."

If I keep rambling long enough, I strategized, maybe there'll be Divine Intervention. But it better come quick. I've already shared the total sum of my knowledge, and time's running out.

"We're reaching thirty seconds," Kingman reminded us.

"Marcy," said Neil, with an unmistakable note of creeping desperation. "I really need your help on this."

I took a deep breath and instantly felt the grip on my hair relax, a sign that my well-founded anxiety was giving way to resignation.

There was someone speaking now. It turned out to be me.

"I'd go with the *Donny and Marie*," I heard myself say. "I just have a feeling."

"A *feeling*? We're talking nearly two million, Marcy. Don't give me *feeling*. Are you sure?"

"Not sure really, Neil, but I think it's a pretty good guess. It has to be one or the other."

Less than a nanosecond later, my spotlight went dark. I sat down again next to my mother, and reached out to hold her hand. The butterflies in my stomach were doing back flips, bouncing around like they had a bad case of attention deficit disorder and had forgotten their medication.

"Time's up," said Kingman. "We've reached that scary juncture: the Moment of Truth. And what a moment for you, Neil. Think over the question carefully one last time, and please give us your answer."

There followed another convulsion of spotlights until it seemed every single one of them landed on Neil, whose face, already drained of color, had taken on the stricken look of a major-party presidential candidate just informed that the networks had changed their minds and were now projecting his opponent to win Florida. The *Filthy Rich!* hot seat never seemed hotter.

My heart, meanwhile, was pounding like one of Desi's congas in the middle of his famous "Babaloo" number, leading to the frantic thought that it might burst right out of my chest, ruining my outfit and requiring Kingman to declare a short time-out to summon an ambulance. That might not be so bad, I reassured myself. The extra time might help Neil come up with the right answer. And I could always buy another outfit.

I'm not particularly big on religion, subscribing as I do to the belief that one bat mitzvah party at Chez Steinberg of Flatbush is joy enough for two or three hundred lifetimes. But with Neil about to cough up his answer, I decided it couldn't hurt to try to enlist some quick help from God. To avoid appearing too craven, I opted against seeking the

Almighty's intervention to make sure Neil won the money. Instead, I silently prayed for the whole thing to be over already. The suspense was inducing cardiac arrhythmia and I'd never gotten around to making out a will.

"If it's your Divine Plan," I told the Lord, "I'm prepared to die young and still unmarried. But please don't make me die young, unmarried, and intestate."

I was about to add that going through probate would be hell on my poor parents when the sound of Neil's voice shut down this introspective round of celestial bargaining.

"Okay, Kingman," Neil decided finally, "I'll go with it. I'll say *Donny and Marie.*"

"Your absolute answer?" Kingman fired back.

"Yes. I'm going with Marcy on this. *Donny and Marie.* She'd better be right."

There was a long pause. At least it seemed long to me. Then came the loud buzzer noise, spelling doom.

"Sorry, Neil and Marcy," Kingman said, sounding genuinely regretful, "the answer is *The Sonny and Cher Comedy Hour.* Too bad. But, Neil, you go home with our thanks for being a great contestant, and—"

Here Kingman broke off. Paying no heed to the genial host, Neil was walking with all deliberate speed in my direction, shouting as he went.

"You bitch. You said you were an expert on old TV shows," he said, temper rising.

"Only classic comedy," I responded, alarmed by Neil's sudden hostility, and what it might portend. "It's what I watched as a kid, and it's the only questions we practiced together for tonight. Classic comedy."

I'd never seen Neil like this before. Then again, I'd never seen the big galoot lose $1.75 million.

Thoroughly caught up in this seamy melodrama, I totally forgot about the TV cameras, which kept rolling right along, capturing all the fast-breaking action. I grabbed my Kenneth Cole shoulder bag off the floor to have it handy for self-defense just in case Neil's demented new agenda included transforming *Filthy Rich!* into *WrestleMania*.

"*Sonny and Cher* was a variety show, Neil," I added firmly. "I know zilch about variety shows. After three years together, you should know that."

"It's a comedy show, goddamn it. Look at the title: *Comedy Hour, Comedy Hour, Comedy Hour.* Only you think it's the *Sonny and Cher Variety Hour.* That's because you never listen. I'm SOOO sick of it, you goddamn witch."

My thoughts raced back to the fun Saturday afternoon when Neil had moved in with me two years ago. I recalled the cozy feeling of couplehood as we struggled to maneuver his prized "thinking chair" to a suitable resting place at the far end of the living room. This heavy monstrosity was actually the dental chair from Neil's first office. He'd had it mounted on a round, stainless-steel pedestal and re-covered in rich, black Corinthian leather—a design decision you either thought was dorky, psychotic, or cute. I chose cute. As they say, love is blind.

"This isn't just mine anymore," I remembered Neil telling me as he stood back to admire the unique piece of

furniture in its brand-new habitat, his right arm affectionately draped over my shoulder. "It belongs to both of us," he
said. To prove he meant it, he then showed me how to adjust
the big foam headrest and which button to press to tilt the
thing back. Afterward, we took a break from moving chores
and made love for the first time as its ostensible co-owners.

The chair was bulky and ugly, and clashed with my pas-
tels. I didn't even think it was that comfortable. But seeing
it there every day made me feel secure. It told me I could
stop worrying about a lonely middle age spent rummaging
for Mr. Right in the crowd standing in line to get into the
Ethical Culture Society singles mixer on alternate Friday
nights. It said I could look forward to wedding bells, and,
someday maybe, the patter of little feet.

Obviously, I had missed something.

"Some Life Coach," Neil ranted. "Anyone who takes
advice from you after this belongs in a goddamn loony bin.
Thanks to your so-called coaching, I've just blown a million
dollars. After taxes!"

Neil then moved on to his next victim, taking a gratu-
itous swipe at my silver-haired and petite sixty-six-year-old
mother, in the process terminally alienating his biggest fan
in my family, and sacrificing any audience sympathy he
might have had left.

"And I can't stand your busybody mother either," Neil
all but screamed at me. "Or her gross, fat-filled cooking.
Her cement matzo balls could turn Elie Wiesel into an anti-
Semite. Every time she cooks her greasy pot roast, it's like

Tinkerbell: Somewhere a bypass surgeon gets a new Mercedes. If you want to give a heart doctor an expensive German car, why not just write a check? If I die before I'm fifty, Marcy, I'm blaming you."

"That makes no sense, Neil, you'll be dead," I replied, injecting a note of logic I hoped would help calm him down. "You won't be around to blame me."

I was trying to lighten things up, but the truth is Neil's pent-up anger came as a shocking and hurtful revelation. So did his expressed hatred of my mother's cuisine, which he did a good job of suppressing for the three years we were together, perhaps because he was so busy shoveling in third and fourth helpings.

"Happy now, Marcy?" Neil resumed sarcastically. "You've ruined my one chance."

"Forget him," my mother shouted back, rising like a phoenix from her chair and seething with all the venom of a Jewish Mother scorned. "You were too good for him anyway." She waved her fist and spit in his general direction.

"Thanks for the support, Mom," I said, expecting her to sit back down. Instead, she was just getting started.

"Look me in the eye," she challenged her former almost-son-in-law-to-be, glaring hard at him. "So this is what we get for treating you like a member of the Mallowitz family? Lies about greasy cooking? Defaming my grandmother's favorite recipes, which her own mother, may she rest in peace, handed down to her back in the old country? You should only live so long to find a more perfect matzo ball, or a cut of brisket to match my delicious pot roast—so lean even that fuddy-duddy stick-in-the-mud Dr. Pritikin would approve. Neil, you should be ashamed."

I was proud of my mother's ferocity, even if mildly perturbed that she'd worked up more steam defending her matzo balls and pot roast than defending her daughter. I hoped no one else would notice.

"*Comedy Hour, Comedy Hour, Comedy Hour,*" Neil repeated, leaning over the low railing that separated the stage from the audience and screaming like a maniac at the top of his lungs.

It's strange what pops into your head at horrible moments like this. What popped into mine at this point was totally frivolous. It was a sweet memory from childhood: Fox's U-Bet Chocolate Flavor Syrup. I wondered if U-Bet still came with a coupon you could mail in for a free pump. I could make Kingman an egg cream. I could make egg creams for the whole audience.

Snapping back to the present, I felt fury beginning to steam through my system. Couldn't Neil have just taken me out to dinner and quietly told me it was over between us? I would have gotten the message. There was no need to trash me and my mother, not to mention my grandmother and great-grandmother by indirection. Nor was there any excuse to attack my professional honor in front of millions of my fellow Americans, including, it was fair to presume, all of my clients, who were either watching the show or would somehow hear about the lively encounter soon afterward.

A Personal Life Coach must inspire confidence to be effective. In addition to hurting my feelings, getting dumped so publicly could not be good for business. As I tend to do when confronted with an unpleasant situation, I asked myself what Marcia Brady, the pretty and generally levelheaded oldest sister on *The Brady Bunch,* would do in a similar fix—a habit derived from repeated exposure at an impressionable age to all the lame *Brady* plots in after-school syndication.

Almost instantly, my inner *Brady* archive referred me to the famous episode where vulnerable teenage Marcia developed a crush on an older man—a tall, handsome dentist whose intentions she totally misread. She managed to get over it in slightly under thirty minutes, including the time for commercials. I know it's fashionable to dismiss Marcia as an obnoxious Little Miss Perfect. But that quality is exactly what makes her a touchstone.

"My mother is right," I blurted out. "I *am* too good for you. *Much* too good. You don't like my answer, Neil? Why don't you go to Hollywood and give this personally to Cher's pal Teri Garr?"

In an uncharacteristically grand gesture, I ripped off the chintzy crystal friendship ring he'd given me as a "pre-engagement present" just before moving into my apartment, and threw it at him as hard as I could. Of course, if this were *The Jerry Springer Show*, probably no one would have noticed. But this was network prime time!

The audience was cheering me now. I think it was heart-felt, although the flashing applause signs made it hard to tell for sure.

At this point, Kingman ambled over from his usual place center stage to help members of the production staff who were frantically trying to pull Neil away before he hurled himself into the audience and succeeded in strangling me, my mother, or the two of us simultaneously, thereby achieving a grisly network first.

Amid this mayhem, the show went to commercial.

"That was great television," the producer said cheerily when the whole thing was over. "Congratulations." He also told me I could look forward to getting paid residuals every time the show aired in reruns.

Call me an ingrate, but under the circumstances, the promise of future residuals was not much consolation. I was no longer sure I had a future.

Years before achieving TV superstardom on *ER*, George Clooney did a brief and unexceptional turn as handyman George Burnett on which long-running sitcom?

a. *Maude*
b. *The Facts of Life*
c. *One Day at a Time*
d. *The Jeffersons*

See correct answer on back. . . .

Two

✦

Okay, come out and say it: Marcy Mallowitz must be a real nitwit to jeopardize a promising long-term relationship by signing on as Neil's Lifeline. This disaster was entirely predictable.

Fair enough. But allow me to say two things in my defense.

1. I agreed to be his Lifeline only under duress. Neil said that if I helped him win the million, he would take it as a sign that we should get married. He further promised that we would honeymoon at an unnamed exotic locale, and, in a departure from all of our previous vacations together, the trip would not coincide in any way with the annual convention of the American Association of Orthodontists, the unrelievedly dreary professional organization to which Neil is totally devoted.

2. It never occurred to me that Neil would actually finagle his way into becoming a *Filthy Rich!* contestant. To be honest, it never occurred to me that Neil's name and the

word "finagle" would ever appear together in the same sentence. I'm totally opposed to stereotypes. But it is well known that orthodontists are better flossers than finaglers. Also, I'm no mind reader. How could I know the show's producers would toss him a dental-related question in the all-important "Fastest Finger of Fate" qualifying round that decides which of the ten candidates flown in from around the country gets a chance to go for the money? It was the show's first dental-trivia question ever.

"Now, group," Kingman said, "for a chance to compete for $1.75 million, rearrange the following well-known national brands of toothpaste in the order in which they were introduced, going from oldest to most recent."

This was the list:

1. Tom's of Maine
2. Colgate
3. Mentadent
4. Crest
5. Pepsodent*

Sitting there helpless in the audience, I knew I was doomed the moment I heard the question. I knew I'd get dragged into this somehow and I wouldn't be able to deliver. I even turned to my mother and said so.

---

*The correct answer, which Neil supplied in a flash, is 1. Colgate; 2. Pepsodent; 3. Crest; 4. Tom's of Maine; and 5. Mentadent.

"I think I'm dead, Mom," I said.

I don't think she heard me. By then, Dear Mom was on her feet applauding Neil's correct answer. That's how quickly he put the toothpastes in order, leaving all of the other would-be contestants in the dust. They didn't even bother to guess.

But, then, Neil had a distinct advantage over the others. Only Neil grew up entertaining his parents' friends at parties by imitating the latest toothpaste commercials, and only he harbored a feverish ambition by the age of four to earn a living shoving his hands in other people's mouths when he grew up. For fun, Neil would organize tongue-twister contests, challenging his school chums to quickly recite Crest's seal of approval from the American Dental Association— "Crest is a decay-preventing dentifrice. . . ." The one who made the fewest mistakes got First Prize.

Neil's precocious interest in diagnosing, correcting, and preventing irregularities of the teeth and poor occlusion led him to develop the strange habit of turning almost every social conversation back to orthodontics. This offended many of my friends, especially one of my two best friends Norma Ruckenhaus, the famous professor of feminist history at New York University who nearly missed getting tenure due to her lengthy procrastination in completing her bestselling treatise *Why Women Don't Achieve as Much as Men.*

"Marcy," Norma said to me after meeting Neil for the first time, "you've got yourself a clunker." The setting for this important debriefing was a small, sticky table in the rear of a crowded Starbucks around the corner from Norma's apartment near Union Square, one of the pretentious java chain's few grungy outposts.

Norma, who is nothing if not outspoken, took a sip from her tiny cup of espresso, and then made a prediction. "If you stay with him, one of two things will happen. You'll end up going back to school to become his dental hygienist. Or, you'll find out that the mysterious lipstick stains on the collar of his starched white dental shirt belong to some glamorous twenty-something chippy whose frequent appointments are not devoted exclusively to making adjustments to her night brace. You won't have to call in Angela Lansbury to solve that caper."

"Okay, Norma, what are you saying," I said, putting down my pricey mug of rejuvenating ginseng orange blossom tea for emphasis, "he's boring or he's having an affair? There seems to be a contradiction."

"I'm saying watch out, kid," Norma said. "I don't trust him."

But, of course, when Norma said "watch out" she hadn't been anticipating Neil's nasty au revoir on network TV, so her qualifications to say "I told you so" are still a matter of debate.

Anyway, Norma's distaste for Neil did not dampen my own enthusiasm. I kept coming up with excuses for his odd behavior, rationalizing that you want the person attaching tortuous contraptions in your mouth to feel totally committed to his line of work. For the most part, I found Neil's devotion to his profession to be endearing. It sounds absurd, I know, but I used to enjoy listening to Neil explain his special method of making sure his clients' upper bicuspids aligned with their lower at the end of treatment. Or to hear him expound on any other orthodontic or dental topic, for that matter, in that soothing baritone of his. He sounded so caring, so knowledgeable and self-assured—and please refrain from laughing when I say this—so sexy. In Neil's casual use of multisyllabic medical terms as he shared insights from the latest literature on overbites, I swear I sometimes heard Doug Ross, George Clooney's dreamy pediatrician character on *ER*.

That is, of course, until our televised dustup shattered my illusions and turned me into the nation's quasi-celebrity of the moment—a "better-bred Buttafuoco" Jay Leno called me the next night in his monologue. "Without the big hair."

Thanks, Jay. And, most of all, thank you, Neil, you crud.

What sitcom's unique Thanksgiving episode involved a scheme to toss live turkeys from a helicopter at 2,000 feet on the mistaken belief that turkeys could fly?

a. *The Beverly Hillbillies*
b. *WKRP in Cincinnati*
c. *Green Acres*
d. *Silver Spoons*

See correct answer on back. . . .

b. *WKRP in Cincinnati*

Three

✦

By the time I dropped my mother off in Brooklyn and returned to Greenwich Village, where I live, the paparazzi were swarming on the sidewalk outside my stately old doorman building. Obviously, the bush telegraph that informs these guys there's a new contender on the scene for the gossip throne previously occupied by Darva Conger, Monica Lewinsky, and their predecessors was already hard at work.

Exiting the taxi, I was blinded by what seemed to be a fifty-megaton flash—the product of several dozen cameramen clicking away in near unison to get the perfect candid shot of yours truly arriving home from her worst nightmare courtesy of *Filthy Rich!*

I was surrounded. From all sides, reporters were barking questions at me. Between the flashes going off, and the microphones being shoved in my face, walking the few feet to enter my building was sort of like scaling Mount Everest without the benefit of a Sherpa.

"Look this way, Marcy."

"How are you feeling?"

"Do you think you'll get back together?"

"What are your plans now?"

"Did you plan to throw the ring, or was it spontaneous?"

"Would you do it again—be your boyfriend's Lifeline if he asked?"

"Would you consider dating another orthodontist?"

Hearing that last question, I was tempted to break my silence, but instead took the revolving door into the lobby, leaving the horde behind.

"I'm so sorry, Miss Mallowitz," the doorman said, as if someone had died and this was a condolence call. He then handed me my dry cleaning.

But before I could make it into the elevator, I was stopped by elderly Mrs. Schwartz, the crabby four-foot-two owner of apartment 7-C. She was heading out to walk her schnauzer, Bruno, who was even crabbier and shorter, and had recently developed the bad habit of peeing on the lobby's oriental carpet.

"Hi there, Marcy," she said with unaccustomed warmth. "You were wonderful. May I have your autograph? I want it to show my mah-jongg group tomorrow."

The request caught me totally off guard. Sure, Mrs. Schwartz and I would exchange pleasantries if we happened to be taking the same elevator. And at a tenant meeting a couple of years ago, I recalled her accusing me and a few other miscreant neighbors of inviting bugs and vermin into the building by failing to adequately seal our plastic garbage bags before dumping them in the basement trash room—a charge to which I pleaded innocent, standing on my honor as an exterminator's daughter. But neither she, nor anyone else, had asked for my autograph since the day they handed out the yearbooks my senior year in high school.

I adjusted the dry cleaning to free my right hand, and dutifully signed "Best Wishes, Marcy Lee Mallowitz" on the back of a small, light-blue appointment card from Mrs. Schwartz's rheumatologist, which she'd excitedly unearthed from her oversize floral purse and handed to me, along with a cheap ballpoint imprinted with the name of a local luncheonette.

"That Kingman Fenimore, don't you just love him?" she said. "What's he really like?"

"Frankly, Mrs. Schwartz, I don't know. I was just a Lifeline. We didn't get much chance to chat."

"That's too bad, dear," she said, pulling on her schnauzer's leash. "I better go now."

Unfortunately, it was too late. While she'd stopped to get my autograph and inquire about Kingman Fenimore, Bruno had left another puddle on the rug. She pretended not to notice and, anxious to take the elevator up to my third-floor one bedroom, so did I.

As soon as I realized my apartment door was unlocked, I could sense that Neil had gotten there ahead of me to clear out his stuff. The nervous churning in my stomach intensi-fied as I put the key back in my purse and stepped inside.

Turning on the lights, I immediately noticed something different about the living room. Neil, the thief, had filched the old dental chair he told me to consider "ours," leaving as his final gift to me the faint skid marks he engraved dragging the bizarre item across the apartment's heavily polyurethaned wood floor. His chair gone, the room seemed suddenly larger and brighter, but also very empty. I stood there for a couple of minutes just staring at the deep indentation left in the corner of the room's plush cream-colored area rug, less upset, I think, than in a state of shock.

It wasn't until a trip to the bathroom that the reality of the breakup actually struck home.

Gone was the cruddy pale-green Water Pik Neil displayed on a specially constructed bathroom shelf, religiously dusting it and explaining that it was a valuable collector's item—a duplicate of one in the Museum of Modern Art's collection.

The old Water Pik was gone, and so was the glass shelf. He'd ripped it out in such a hurry, there were big holes in the plaster. I'd have to fix them myself now without the benefit of the special dental-mold plaster Neil used to bring home from work for such household repairs.

Left behind, though, was at least one tangible souvenir of my three-year fling with a man whose love for the dental arts turned out to be a lot more enduring than whatever he felt for me. There, at their regular berth by the bathroom sink, gleaming in the artificial light of the overhead fluorescent, were the "His" and "Hers" water squirters Neil had ordered from his dental-supply place. He had them installed as a surprise for me on our first anniversary together.

What a romantic evening that was. After a candlelit dinner at a small French bistro in the Village, we walked the few blocks back to my cozy third-floor apartment at Tenth Street and Fifth Avenue holding hands and sucking on the special sugar-free breath mints Neil always brought along for after meals. We said good night to the doorman, and once upstairs Neil led me wordlessly to the john to show me his gift, which the building's handyman had installed while we were gone.

"Here's to us, Marcy," Neil said, raising the sprayer marked "His." I picked up the one marked "Hers" and we knocked ends as Neil offered a touching, if somewhat peculiar, toast. I now realize it probably wasn't original, only a pickup line he learned in dental school, but at the time it seemed heartfelt: "The couple that spritzes together, fits together."

How Neil loved those squirters. They were just like the ones he used with patients, except the home version didn't have the capacity to blow air, he would explain to guests, always insisting they not leave the bathroom without sampling the soothing warm-water spray laced with a special mouthwash of Neil's choosing—his "flavor of the month," he called it.

Somehow Neil missed the social cues that would inform a normal person that the guest he had followed into the bathroom preferred to relieve himself in peace without first being lectured about the undeniable virtues of Neil's spritzers.

When my friends and I had a girls' night out, Norma would draw big guffaws by imitating Neil's awkward way of breaking the ice whenever he met new people.

"Hey," he'd say, typically interrupting the conversation, "did you wear braces as a kid? I'm just asking because you have an interesting bite."

Having heard all of this, you're probably asking yourself what an otherwise sane, not unattractive Barnard alumna like myself possibly saw in a conceitedly decent-looking thirty-five-year-old man so plainly obsessed with his power to move other people's teeth.

As I've said, I wasn't blind to Neil's flaws. But until his bad behavior on *Filthy Rich!*, I thought him sweet, and told myself his excessive fondness for his profession, while a tad unusual, maybe, was a small price to pay for keeping alive what could be my only hope of getting married and having a family.

My codependent in this was my mother, who persistently plied Neil with her special potato latkes and home-made applesauce like he was the Second Coming, based in part on a mistaken notion about the exact nature of his degree.

"Everyone's kvelling!" my mother would regularly exclaim, apropos of nothing. "My daughter, the Barnard graduate, is marrying a doctor."

"Well, Mom," I'd say, "you got one out of three right. That's not bad."

Do the scoring yourself. It was true I went to Barnard, blue-ribbon class of '89. But Neil hadn't proposed, and he's only an orthodontist, not a real medical doctor.

My mother would not be moved. "So, what's wrong with an orthodontist? *New York* magazine says he's one of the best, and if I may quote, 'one of the innovators in the use of clear-plastic bite plates that do the work of braces while minimizing the embarrassing appearance problems.'"

She carried the clipping around in her purse. As far as my mother was concerned, Neil's early experimentation with plastic braces put him in the elite vanguard of modern science, in a league with Louis Pasteur or, even better, Paul Muni, her favorite movie star as a kid, who, as she's fond of imparting, acted in Yiddish theater before gaining Oscar immortality by portraying the great French chemist and bacteriologist in the inspiring 1936 Hollywood biography. When I was ten, my mother let me stay up until 3 A.M. with her to catch it on a local channel's late-movie show airing in the wee hours now filled by paid infomercials for the amazing Ab Roller. My failure to swoon over Mr. Muni and his overacting remains a sore point to this day, and our discussions of the matter always end the same way—with my mother declaring I can't really be her daughter, and that there must have been a mix-up at the hospital.

But what really sealed my mom's case for Neil was his title. "And look here, my smarty girl," she'd say, pointing to some tiny type in her pawed-over clipping. "They call him *Dr.* Postit. That's good enough for me."

My mother's desire for me—her pampered only child—to marry a doctor was not a casual thing. When I started pushing the Big Three-Oh with no promising prospects in sight, Mom sprang into action. She started spending less time with her empty-nest housewife friends in Midwood, the middle-class Brooklyn neighborhood where I grew up, and took a volunteer job in the gift shop at Long Island Jewish Medical Center, all with the uncharitable motive of finding yours truly an eligible man-in-white. She didn't have any luck until the unsuspecting Dr. Abramowitz, internal medicine, happened into the store to buy a newspaper and let himself be cashiered into a blind date. It was a long, awkward evening, although I did learn something about the possible dangerous side effects of certain herbal remedies unregulated by the Food and Drug Administration. Never again, I vowed, would I allow myself to fall victim to my mother's matchmaking—a stance, incidentally, that was fully supported by my normally above-the-fray father, Herbert Mallowitz, the hardworking owner of Brooklyn Roach Patrol, a successful extermination company. He has survived harmoniously with my mother all these years by being the only human more relaxed than Ozzie Nelson in the old TV series I watched in reruns as a kid. My dad even wears cardigan sweaters like Ozzie's.

Actually, in the interest of full disclosure, my father has one decidedly un-Ozzie-like quirk. He enjoys razzing my mother about her spending habits by translating the dollar

amount of her store purchases into a dead-roach count—
that is, his estimate of the number of the disgusting bugs his
firm will need to kill in order to cover the price tag.

"So what do you think, Herbie?" my mother will say,
modeling a new dress she picked up on sale at a little bou-
tique on Kings Highway opened by some entrepreneurial
Russian immigrants.

"I think I better fetch my sprayer" is Dad's stock answer,
which only he finds humorous. "For that pretty number
you have on, I'd calculate it's curtains for fifteen hundred
roaches, give or take. But for you, Frannie, anything. Wear it
in good health."

The official family shorthand for this tiresome one-joke
drill is "The Dead Roach Routine," as in "Herbie, spare
me, please, not your Dead Roach Routine again!"

Anyway, it wasn't long after the Dr. Abramowitz fiasco that
I started going out with Neil.

Except for one brief, awkward moment at the tail end of
an introductory Sunday brunch at a choice table in the
Molly Picon Room at the Second Avenue Deli, Mom
always thought Neil was the greatest. That awkward
moment occurred when Neil, sensitive soul that he is, dis-
closed in response to her prodding that the reason he didn't
get down to Miami much to visit his parents at their retirement community was because he was "really busy," and
because it bothered him "to be around a lot of old people

with dentures." My mother's jaw dropped, revealing a big piece of unchewed prune Danish I thought she might spit in his eye. But after I kicked Neil hard under the table, he quickly recovered, reassuring Mom in his sweetest voice that he really loved his parents, and that he had nothing against elderly people or their teeth. He also told my mother her own teeth were particularly lovely, and drew her into an absorbing chat about her use of Arm & Hammer baking soda every other day to help keep them white and youthful-looking. Sticking to this very confined subject area, Neil could be pretty compelling when he turned on the charm.

After that, Neil could do no wrong as far as my mother was concerned. And it always seemed to me that Neil felt pretty much the same way about her, reserving his warmest feelings (notwithstanding his pathetic attempt at revisionist history) for her hearty, home-cooked dishes, especially the brisket. For the record, he also loved her stuffed cabbage. Just not as much.

Indeed, it seemed Mom was the only family member Neil didn't alienate when, not long after that brunch, he held up my family's Passover Seder an excruciating twenty-five minutes in order to muddle, turtlelike, through the Four Questions in Hebrew. People around the table tried to persuade Neil to cease and desist, making the powerful argument that little Rachel, my cousin Lisa's adorable six-year-old, had just covered the very same questions in English, and absent evidence of intentional fraud or tampering, that version should be considered definitive. But my bullheaded, tone-deaf boyfriend insisted on plodding ahead, cheerfully oblivious to the impression he was making on family members, most of whom he was meeting for the first time, and the vehemence of their registered objections.

"Keep your shirts on, guys," Neil told them with a friendly smile. "I just want to see if I can do this. We'll get to Moses and the Red Sea in a jiffy, I promise. Besides, the chicken soup isn't going to run away if the Seder takes a couple of extra minutes. At least it never has before. That I know of."

Rather than blame Neil for this bone-headed hijacking, however, I blamed myself. I should have warned him, I thought as he laboriously rounded what I assumed was the Third Question since he was flashing three fingers. The Mallowitz family has very definite ideas about how to celebrate Passover, and one of the most definite is that a leisurely bilingual retelling of our people's deliverance from Egyptian bondage is only for sissies and the Orthodox. In my progressive family, a Seder means a speedy but respectful revisiting of a few essential high points as succinctly retold in worn Maxwell House Haggadahs that were a supermarket freebie back when Charlton Heston had real hair, and still dearly treasured as the enduring Gold Standard for accelerating arrival at everyone's favorite part of the evening—the part when we eat.

Eventually, Neil achieved his dubious goal of completing the Four Questions in Hebrew. "Yes!" he shouted, punching one hand in the air, as if pissing off my famished relatives on an important Jewish holiday was some kind of major Olympic event. However, even his bombast could not revive ancient Great-Aunt Beatrice, who by then had fallen sound asleep. Her blue-haired head was resting on a damp section of tablecloth near her plate, where someone had earlier accidentally spilled their glass of Manischewitz, and she was snoring loudly.

My mother, on the other hand, seemed nearly as impressed by Neil's offensive linguistic feat as the handsome lad himself. Looking at my mother looking at Neil struggle with Hebrew letters he hadn't seen or thought about since his bar mitzvah more than twenty years before, I could tell exactly what she was thinking, even if I was a little lost by her logic: If there's anything finer for my Marcy than a handsome and successful Jewish orthodontist, it's a handsome and successful Jewish orthodontist who can recite the Four Questions in Hebrew. Now there's a catch!

Determined to do nothing that might jinx my prospects with this "find," Mom bit her tongue when I violated Mallowitz Moral Law, handed down through the ages, by letting Neil move in with me without getting married, and, even more dismaying from Mom's standpoint, before any formal engagement. Instead of expressing her displeasure, she tried to be encouraging, buying us our own new brass mezuzah, for example, to replace the old, blackened one hung outside the door by previous occupants. "Every couple should have their own," she said, reaching mysteriously into her handbag to pull out a hammer and nail brought from home to tack the thing up. Predictably, dear Mom also brought with her a large foil package of the baked brisket Neil fell for that crazy Seder night. Indeed, his affection for my mother's brisket was such that I sometimes thought he loved her tender, well-seasoned beef more than he loved me, that is, if he ever *really* loved me at all, which is something I would no longer wager my little Palm Pilot Vx on.

Mom's fondness for Neil extended to making excuses for the chintzy crystal ring Neil bestowed on me as a so-called preengagement gift even after my low-key father gave it a withering dead-roach count that amounted to calling Neil cheap.

"No spraying needed for this thing," said Dad matter-of-factly, looking over the ring on my hand and slowly shaking his head at the stinginess of Neil's gesture. "The roaches are safe."

"Herbie, be quiet," my mother ordered. "You're just still ticked off about the Seder. Neil's love for Marcy isn't something that can be measured in roaches. Besides, he's probably saving up to buy her a fabulous engagement ring."

But, of course, all of this was before the acrimonious finale of *Filthy Rich!*, which famously concluded with me chucking the insulting bauble back in Neil's face.

Glancing now at the two spritzers in the bathroom we once shared, I was overcome with a wave of sadness. Face it, I said to myself, he's not coming back.

I was unsure about a lot of things, but not this: Due to a

regrettable but not typically life-threatening deficit in my knowledge about Sonny and Cher's Hour of Yucks, or whatever that damned show was called, I would never be Mrs. Neil Postit.

Distracted, I picked up the "Hers" spritzer the wrong way, accidentally pressing down its trigger, to send a warm, thin stream of water cascading down the big mirror in back of the sink. The effect was surreal. It was if the room itself was weeping at Neil's departure, calling into question my own lack of tears.

I wandered aimlessly into the kitchen. After three years together—during more than two of which he was calling my mother "Mom"—there was no good-bye note. Just house keys tossed casually on the Formica counter on the way out the door with all his clothing, his bulky thinking chair, and his beloved vintage dental appliance.

Bone weary from my momentous evening, I got myself ready to go to sleep. I put on an old ratty flannel nightgown Neil despised and made sure both my regular phone and cell phone were shut off. I didn't want my much-needed beauty rest interrupted by calls from well-meaning friends and family members wanting to commiserate with my nationally televised launch into loserhood.

Then I did something totally subversive—something I didn't dare do when Neil was around. I went to bed without flossing.

In one memorable episode of *The Jeffersons*, George Jefferson finally persuades his son, Lionel, to join the family business. What was the business?

a. A chain of fast-food restaurants
b. A chain of discount appliance stores
c. A chain of dry-cleaning shops
d. A big auto dealership

See correct answer on back. . . .

A N S W E R

✦

c. A chain of dry-cleaning shops

Four

✦

One maddening thing that happens when you collide with fame is that people who have never met you, will never meet you, and don't even particularly care to meet you suddenly have nothing better to do than engage in misleading and inaccurate speculation about who you really are. They invent childhood traumas, colorful relatives, drug and drinking issues, and love affairs and one-night stands more numerous and passionate than even Bill Clinton has experienced. Sometimes these false accounts take on a life of their own.

Contrary to the widespread rumor, for example, I did not decide to become a Personal Life Coach because my first career as a member of a traveling troupe of exotic dancers was in a rut. Nor did I experience a spiritual awakening while playing the ukulele topless in a half-filled theater in Dubuque. Indeed, when that rumor first appeared in *People,* I penned an angry letter explaining that I've never been an exotic dancer or in danger of visiting Dubuque. The magazine didn't run it, which I suppose is just as well, since it's doubtful anyone would have paid attention in the midst of the mad feeding frenzy that immediately followed my abrupt and completely unwarranted rise to fame.

Having finally dispelled the exotic dancer rumor, I'll endeavor to solve the mystery of how I ended up becoming a Personal Life Coach. I can sum up the answer in one word: closets.

After college, when most of my classmates were entering graduate school or beginning to make their way on Wall Street, I struck out in a different direction. Within hours of striding up the aisle to claim my Barnard diploma amid thunderous applause from an appreciative audience packed with dozens of Mallowitzes and assorted family hangers-on from as far away as Toledo, I was sitting at the kitchen table at my family's house in Brooklyn, earnestly perusing the help wanted ads in the Sunday *New York Times.*

Every few minutes or so, my father would come by in his bathrobe, feigning interest in getting "a nibble" from the refrigerator, and then resume his hard lobbying to get me to enter the family business.

"Why are you going to work for strangers, Marcy, when we could be working together? We'd be a great team. Remember how much fun you used to have going out with me on jobs?"

"Sure I had fun, Dad," I'd reply. "Why wouldn't I? I was four years old."

"To me, Marcy, you'll always be my little girl. But your

old man isn't getting any younger. In a couple years, you could be running the whole show. We can change the name right away: 'Marcy's Roach Patrol,' starting tomorrow. I'll even repaint our trucks. Any color you want. Except pink or purple. And not aqua blue. That's for richies in Manhattan. What do you think?"

"Dad, I love you," I kept telling him, "but I don't want to run an exterminating business. Besides, I'd insist on aqua blue. Trucks *and* uniforms. You'd kick me out in a second, and Mom would have to make something up to tell the relatives."

"Maybe you're right," he'd answer, seemingly convinced, only to keep returning to the kitchen to repeat his pitch. But I wasn't going to let my dad's well-meaning interruptions deter me.

There was no shortage of opportunities for someone burning to be a computer programmer or part-time legal secretary. Ditto for those yearning to teach high school algebra or enter the exciting field of private security. Naturally, I skipped right past. This was my Future, and I had my standards. I wanted a challenging position with plenty of room for upward mobility. It had to come with a salary big enough to pay the rent, and even bigger psychic rewards. More than simply earning a living, I was determined to fulfill the burning ambition I've harbored as far back as Mrs. Feldbaum's eye-opening eighth-grade civics class. I wanted to put my talents to work helping people.

For a long time, I hoped to do that by becoming a psychologist, which I thought, perhaps simplistically, was a whole lot cooler than becoming a full-fledged psychiatrist, because you get to do more or less the same thing without the expense and tedium of having to go to medical school or traipse around depressing hospitals all night wearing cloddy rubber-soled shoes. My mother, who harbors no respect for the mental-health profession owing to a longtime antipathy to Dr. Joyce Brothers, did her best to try to convince me to become a schoolteacher instead, like Mrs. Feldbaum.

"If you want to get married and have children," Francine Mallowitz summarily pronounced, "teaching is the only way to go." As my erudite mom saw it, Sigmund Freud was just "a lot of mumbo-jumbo hocus-pocus."

Nothing I said could dissuade her. Mom's know-nothing view of Freud was set in stone years ago by a single casual viewing of the strange movie in which the legendary shrink was played by Montgomery Clift, who was by then pretty strange himself. No doubt if Paul Muni's Hollywood oeuvre included a bio-epic of Freud to match his Louis Pasteur and Émile Zola, my mother's attitude would have been entirely different.

In the end, however, my decision to give up on psychology had nothing to do with my mother or her dubious taste in movie actors. It was based on a realistic assessment that my middling science grades, combined with two years of marks in statistics rumored to be among the lowest ever recorded by the college, doomed my chances of being accepted by any decent psychology graduate program. By that I mean a program sufficiently respectable for me to stand a chance of ever earning enough money to repay the sizable loans I'd need to take out in order to attend.

My parents had footed the bill entirely for college, and I wasn't going to drain their savings further to underwrite some psychology pipe dream—not that they didn't offer. As for the smallish nest egg left to me by my grandparents, my plan was to wait until the housing market softened a bit, and I had a good, steady job, and then use it as a down payment on an apartment in Manhattan, which is just what I eventually did.

I was disappointed to forgo a graduate degree, but hardly heartbroken. By senior year, I'd grown tired of school and was impatient to venture forth into the Real World to seek my Destiny.

After perusing the *Times* employment section for half an hour, I came across an intriguing recruitment ad on the back page for a young California company seeking to expand in New York City. I got a goose-bumpy feeling. *This might be it!*

When the office opened its doors the next morning at 9 A.M., I was already waiting outside to obtain an interview. An hour later, I was an employee of Santa Monica Spaces, an outfit that dispatches its enthusiastic minions to *help people* organize their closets. *Eureka!* Barely a day out of college, and I had met my goal of securing a meaningful berth in a helping profession, albeit one with the undignified motto "Have Hanger, Will Travel."

My mother wasn't pleased. She reacted to the happy

news of her daughter's employment as if it were a dastardly plot against her hatched by some satanic sitcom creators in Hollywood.

"You're going to do *what?*" she greeted me with upon my triumphant return from the job interview. "For this we scrimped and saved to send you to a fancy-schmancy college? To clean people's closets? Tell me the truth, Marcy, this is your *Brady Bunch* lunacy, isn't it? I could have predicted. I remember, you always liked their maid, you know, whatsername, Hazel. Now you're trying to be like her."

"Alice," I said. "Mom, the name of the Bradys' maid was Alice. And for your information, she was probably my *least favorite* character. I just felt sorry for her because the family made her wear a uniform and do all the housework while everyone else lazed around in bell bottoms and polyester leisure suits. It aroused my sense of social injustice."

"So now it's my fault for playing you Pete Seeger?"

"Mom, this isn't about Pete Seeger. And liking *The Brady Bunch* in all its shallow, tacky glory just puts me in the American mainstream. My devotion may be a bit excessive, I admit. But it's just a goofy hobby, like some people carve little sculptures out of Ivory soap to relax. It has nothing to do with my working for Santa Monica Spaces."

"Okay, Marcy, you win. Do what you want. I'm just going to lie and tell the family you're a junior executive with Sara Lee. If someone gets nosy and starts asking questions, I'll say you're working on their new line of frozen blintzes. Very high finance. You're selling stock."

"Do they even make blintzes?" I inquired.

"So suddenly I'm Sara Lee Mallowitz?" Mom replied, demonstrating her own distinctive version of the Socratic method. "How the hell do I know?"

Fortunately, my fictitious career with Sara Lee didn't last long. Less than two weeks after this conversation occurred, I took some of my hard-earned salary and paid to have my mother's cramped bedroom closet outfitted with nifty new shelves, racks, and bins from Santa Monica Spaces. The whole works! Mom was so bowled over by the improvement, she called Aunt Gertie in Woodmere, and demanded she drive to Brooklyn right away to see what her "genius daughter" had done. "It's a miracle," she declared. "My clothes have room to breathe again."

For the next three years, my life was a dizzying blur of fancy apartments, messy shoe piles, overcrowded clothing racks, haphazard shelving filled with useless, dust-covered tchotchkes, and profound conversations about the fears, disappointments, and aspirations of my female clients. My sessions with clients frequently turned deeply personal, as talk about dysfunctional sock drawers led them to share deeper concerns about dysfunctional relationships and job situations.

In time, then, I came to see their closets not as mere storage space, but as a metaphor for their untidy, and ultimately unfulfilling, existence. Inspired by a motivational infomercial by Tony Robbins I happened to catch on a night of Diet Coke–induced insomnia, I immodestly decided I had the personal capacity to help my clients clean up both—their closets and the quality of their lives. No longer content confining myself to advising clients on how to rearrange their shirt bins, I now wanted to assist them in rearranging their priorities and taking control of their lives.

Muscling past my fears and insecurities, I took action, negotiating a friendly parting of the ways with Santa Monica Spaces to devote myself full-time to building a new career as a Personal Life Coach, or Personal Coach, as many of my colleagues in this fast-bourgeoning segment of the self-realization and personal-growth industry like to call themselves. I choose to insert the word "Life" in my coaching description to clearly delineate the assistance I offer from the overrated but extravagantly compensated "executive coaching" that has lately become standard to improve the leadership skills of top corporate talent and enhance the functioning of the businesses they run. I also think Personal Life Coach sounds peppier.

In a sense, I suppose, my evolving focus from vexing closet issues to a fuller intervention in people's lives as a Personal Life Coach was not surprising given my early interest in psychology. Yet, for the sake of clarity and to avoid potential lawsuits, I want to underscore that I am not a therapist practicing without a license, as Kingman Fenimore jocularly implied. My decidedly *un*-Freudian coaching does not process the client's emotional history or diagnose or treat mental-health issues. I call my sessions "Marcy's Can-Do Hour" because the whole point is to focus on the present and what specific, practical steps the client can take to get unstuck from her present circumstances and achieve the change she wants to make in her life. I have little patience for weepy complainers. My approach is direct and concrete, a mixture of tough love and tough shove.

The worst thing about being a Personal Life Coach is that people at cocktail parties inevitably ask, "What sport?" when you tell them what you do for a living. Another bad thing is that you're competing with a lot of charlatans who have never received coach training, or passed the International Coach Federation's certification exam, and who nevertheless insist on using ridiculous non-verbs like "transitioning, partnering, and career-pathing" and inserting them in pretentious, full-color brochures marketing their services. It gives my profession a bad name.

The best thing about Life Coaching is the opportunity it provides to meet new people, which naturally brings me to the subject of how I met Neil.

I was retained by a client, Jane McDee, the wanly pretty twenty-four-year-old heiress to a vast fast-food fortune, who spoke so quietly I instinctively reached to turn up my hearing aid the first time we spoke, and then realized I don't wear one.

Jane had two problems she wanted to address. By the way, neither related to the dark roots that poked out embarrassingly from her otherwise impressive crop of long blond hair, which I thought a shame because I know a great colorist to whom I've referred any number of other client-victims of Nice 'n Easy do-it-yourself jobs. Anyway, Jane, who wore a colorful headband to keep her hair from falling in her face, tended to favor denim capris and tight, cropped shirts that exposed more than her midriff, a fashion statement that practically screamed Britney Spears and suggested no one had broken the news to the hamburger princess that her teen years were over.

The reason she sought coaching was that she had reached her wits' end trying to figure out how to store her extensive bandanna collection to provide easy access and minimize wrinkles. Also, she was tired of never smiling because she was embarrassed by her giant buck teeth. The bandanna issue I could easily solve on my own. For the tooth question, I did a quick search of recent dental-related stories in *The New York Times,* most of which contained extensive quotes from Neil Postit, who was identified in the articles as a prominent New York City orthodontist with a practice strictly confined to treating adults.

More intrepid research—I dialed information and asked—produced Neil's office phone number. I called and made an appointment to consult with him about Jane's case.

We bonded instantly. Maybe it was just the powerful physical attraction. Or maybe it's because we're both tidy types who broadcast enthusiasm about our work. The right answer is probably all of the above.

Our first real date, an all-day excursion to the Hamptons on a sunny Saturday in early April, weeks before the summer crush, left me convinced that Neil and I also shared the same outlook on life. We drove around the posh Georgica Pond area, where Steven Spielberg and Martha Stewart have their spreads, gawking at the giant houses with their gorgeous landscaping, and making jokes about the sick values of a community where the *average* house goes for several million, you need to be famous to get weekend reservations in a decent restaurant, the official family car is a fully loaded Lexus SUV, and the toy du jour is a high-tech device that allows drivers stuck in never-ending traffic on the Long Island Expressway to turn on the hot tub with a call from the cell phone.

In retrospect, I was so anxious to conclude that Neil was Dr. Right that I overlooked the signs that our values were really very different. Actually, I was the one making all the jokes and providing the negative cultural commentary on money and celebrity run amok that day in the Hamptons. Neil didn't say much. He was too busy gawking, and I've since come to think, longing to party with Alec Baldwin and Christie Brinkley and the rest of the rich and glamorous Hamptons set.

But, as I said, I had blinders on. They were still on more than two years later, when *Filthy Rich!* first went on the air, emerging as a TV phenomenon, and Neil, newly obsessed with the idea of becoming a contestant, started exhibiting some odd behavior.

He began keeping a meticulously catalogued videotape library of every show, and then proceeded to watch his favorites over and over on nights no new segment of *Filthy Rich!* was on the schedule. Where previously he'd run on about dental matters, Neil now provided extensive quotes from the hot game show when we went out to dinner with other couples, which he awkwardly interspersed with random pieces of trivia culled from an eclectic assortment of newly acquired atlases and world almanacs. He also purchased three dozen copies of Kingman Fenimore's autobiography to hand out to patients, and had his secretary leave big blanks in his appointment book so he could keep calling the special 800 number for phone tryouts that could lead to a shot at the *Filthy Rich!* hot seat. The limit was two calls a day, but the line was always busy, Neil explained, and sometimes he'd defy the limit by using aliases. His favorite was Max Flax. For some reason, Neil was always amused by names that rhymed.

Probably I should have been alarmed by his odd transformation. But when it began, I didn't see anything terribly amiss. To be entirely candid, I was just happy Neil had found something other than orthodontics that really interested him. I now suspect that I was also subconsciously afraid that if I began probing much into the mystery behind Neil's new *Filthy Rich!* obsession, I might not like what I found.

What deep inner hunger was it that had Neil so upended? Was it simply monetary greed? A secret yearning for a big career change? Or was it the chance for momentary fame that intrigued him? In future years, cultural experts who study the societal impact of *Filthy Rich!* may come up with a definitive answer. While they're at it, I suppose, they may also tell us whether Certs is really a breath mint or a candy.

Personally, I can't wait.

After playing Richie Cunningham's mom on *Happy Days*, actress Marion Ross perfected a Yiddish accent to convincingly portray a Jewish grandmother on another weekly take on the 1950s, the much-acclaimed *Brooklyn Bridge*. What was the grandmother's name?

a. Sophie Berger
b. Molly Goldberg
c. Golda Levine
d. Selma Silverman

See correct answer on back. . . .

```
ANSWER

✦

a. Sophie Berger
```

Five

◆

I was awakened by the dulcet tones of Frank, the morning doorman, alternately yelling my name, ringing my doorbell, and pounding on my apartment door.

"Ms. Mallowitz, Ms. Mallowitz, are you okay?" he shouted.

"Yeah, I guess so," I replied, still lying in bed, and in the process of trying to prop open my right eyelid with an index finger.

"What's that? Is that you, Ms. Mallowitz?"

"Yes, Frank. It's me, unfortunately. You can stop banging."

I threw on a terry bathrobe and plodded to the door in a bleary state located somewhere between dead and don't bother to resuscitate.

"Some rough night," Frank blurted out when he saw me, which I took to be as much a commentary on my disheveled appearance as the dire doings on *Filthy Rich!* "Your mom was getting worried because your phone was shut off, so she called downstairs and asked me to check on you. She says she left a message on your machine you should play back right away."

"Tell me, Frank, what time is it?"

"Almost ten o'clock."

For my mother, the early bird, waiting until 10 A.M. showed remarkable restraint. She thinks nothing of calling at 6 or 7 A.M. when she has one of her brainstorms, as if saying she didn't mean to wake me makes waking me okay.

"If she calls again, Frank, do me a favor and lie. Tell her you saw me and I looked just fine."

"Sure thing," he said. "Oh, and I almost forgot. These flowers came for you. Two gigantic arrangements. Almost identical. From the same fancy Upper East Side florist. I took them up with me on the service elevator. Wait, I'll fetch them."

An enormous feeling of relief came over me. Of course, I assumed the flowers were from Neil. After all, it wouldn't be the first time he'd resorted to sending flowers when he wanted to apologize for something and couldn't think of an appropriate dental item.

Frank carried the mega-floral offerings to my kitchen counter and departed. I saw a little white card Scotch-taped to one of them, and I snatched it, fully expecting it to contain one of Neil's schmaltzy messages, telling me, as he did once last year, that "Our fight last night left a cavity-size hole in my heart" or something equivalently gruesome. We'd get back together, and life would go on as before. At least that's what I hoped would happen, or thought I hoped.

But never mind the speculation. The card was not from Neil, and there was no mention of a cavity-size anything. It was from Barbara Walters. She'd seen my *Filthy Rich!* gig and wanted me for an exclusive interview.

I'll say that again in case you weren't paying attention: BARBARA WALTERS! The legendary ABC newswoman who interviewed Monica Lewinsky, and no shortage of other major and mini-celebrities, wanted to talk to *me*.

"Dear Marcy," her card said, "Admired your fortitude on *Filthy Rich!* You have a story to share with American women, and I'd like to help you do it. Feel free to call me at home, 555-5094. Your friend, Barbara Walters."

The second group of flowers was from Barbara's arch competitor at ABC, Diane Sawyer.

My God, I thought, DIANE SAWYER! Among her many other journalistic coups, she did the big interview with Darva Conger. That was the exclusive where Darva, the big phony, somberly lamented her loss of privacy and credibility shortly after she married a stranger for money on live TV, and just before she agreed to pose nude for *Playboy*. "The pictures," Darva later explained, "have a feeling of innocence." Yeah, sure.

Diane Sawyer's friendly note gave me her home phone number, offered two passes to the opening of a new movie the next month by her director husband, Mike Nichols, and invited me and a guest to sit at their table at the opening-night party.

My first reaction was to feel flattered by the attention

from these two famous television journalists. After all, I'm only human. But within an hour, the initial excitement wore off, and I was feeling even more depressed than before. In my one appearance on national television, I had managed to make a fool of myself and lose the man I thought I'd marry. I had no desire to stage a television return in order to share more of my personal travails with the motley group of strangers who comprise the viewing public. This fame thing is vastly overrated. Besides, I couldn't get past the question of who I would bring as a guest to Diane Sawyer's soiree since Neil was no longer a possibility.

My quiet but secure existence as an obscure Personal Life Coach attached to a boring orthodontist with a monster-size ego was over. The looming challenge was coming to terms with that fact.

I pressed the playback button on my answering machine.

"Marcy, it's your mother."

Who else would I think it was?

"Everybody's kvelling," she said, obviously recovered from the demeaning events of the previous night. "You made the front page of the *New York Post.* You have to see it. You're throwing the ring at that bastard Neil, and you look fabulous. That outfit we picked up at the Saks sale does wonders for your figure."

I had reached rock bottom, my life was falling apart to such a degree that I felt as if I might never leave my apartment again, and all my mother seemed to care about was how thin I looked in the pictures.

That's Mom. I could be arrested for crimes against humanity and her only comment would be how good I looked in the mug shot. A case of misplaced values or simple maternal loyalty? You make the call.

"And, dear, you'll love the headline: 'Marcy to Neil: Drop Dead.' It's all over TV, too. You know Matt Lauer, the adorable young man on the *Today* show? He talked about you today with the weatherman. You know, that big guy with the earmuffs who's always out there in the cold with the tourists, whatsisname, Al Roker. He said Neil's a nerd and it's not your fault you missed the Sonny and Cher question. Who'd want to be friends with someone who keeps track of Teri Garr's comings and goings? Listen carefully to me, Marcy, that Matt Lauer, I know he's married. But maybe he has a brother. Get one of your well-connected friends to find out. Tell her it's okay even if he's a couple of years younger. Why be a stickler? Call me later."

Click.

The next message was from my friend Norma, just returned from a whirlwind national book tour promoting her trail-blazing new collection of essays on current feminist issues, *Raging Hormones and Other Outrages.*

"Sorry, Marcy," she said. "But I told you so."

What was the name of Rhoda Morgenstern's heard-but-never-seen doorman on the *Mary Tyler Moore Show* spinoff *Rhoda*?

a. Bradley
b. Charles
c. Carlton
d. Fred

See correct answer on back. . . .

ANSWER

✦

c. Carlton

Six

✦

The flowers from Barbara Walters and Diane Sawyer were just the beginning. By four o'clock of The Day After, poor Frank and his afternoon counterpart, hunky Jonathan, heartthrob of the building's over-sixty set, had made at least a dozen deliveries to my apartment—all gifts from prominent people I'd never met trying to ingratiate themselves with Marcy now that she'd been rejected by her obnoxious orthodontist.

Think about that for a moment. People who less than a day before wouldn't have bothered to give me the right, or even the wrong, time of day, for that matter, were now plying me with choice items charged to their expense accounts all because another person they knew only by his unappealing television performance decided he was too good for me. Bizarre, no?

But even more bizarre from my standpoint was the odd, floating sensation all of this largesse induced in me. I can't remember all of the gifts, which I sincerely regret because I really should have appreciated the care that went into each and every card and present. But I do recall the giant Godiva assortments sent by Katie Couric, Bryant Gumbel, Maury Povich, and Larry King as bribes to try to get me to agree to an interview. I remember them mainly because I ended up eating every precious morsel the boxes contained, breaking my personal record for chocolate consumption—part of a sickening three-day binge that did nothing to restore the self-esteem badly damaged by Neil's bad behavior, but did succeed in adding seven unsightly pounds of pure flab to what the *Daily News* had previously described as my "compact but not pudgy athletic frame."

Montel's shipment of giant hand-dipped strawberries from Dean & Deluca also hit the spot, but endeavoring to trick my fat cells, I overlooked their thick bittersweet-chocolate coating and counted them as fruit.

The generous gift basket of assorted gourmet salamis and cheeses from Balducci's, the fancy Village food shop, didn't do any wonders for my waistline either. It came with a lovely card from Tina Brown, the powerhouse editor whose trendy magazine, *Talk,* has tons of financing from Harvey Weinstein at Miramax, and is *the* source for fascinating scoops about his films. "Marcy, you were riveting," she scribbled hastily, possibly on her way to one of those gaudy celebrity shindigs she's always tossing on a yacht. "Can you do lunch next week, just the two of us and Gwyneth? I'm thinking our next cover with a movie tie-in. Have to run, Tina."

Gwyneth Paltrow might play *me* in the movies? Does that mean I get to meet Ben Affleck? I wondered. Then I got worried. They better not cast him as Neil. He'd be too sympathetic.

Tom Brokaw sent no salamis. But he did send me a hand-written letter tendering an invitation to his Montana ranch if I'd appear on his *NBC Nightly News* broadcast. There was also an autographed boxing glove from Geraldo, inscribed "Round One to Marcy," Hostess Ding Dongs, Twinkies, and an incredibly soft and comfortable jogging suit in pale pink from Rosie O'Donnell, and a large canvas public tele-vision tote bag from Charlie Rose filled with videotapes of opera highlights from *This Evening at the Met*. I confess I don't like opera, but the fact that Charlie Rose believed I was sufficiently highbrow to like opera won him my loyalty forever. As for Rosie's jogging suit with the tastefully small imprint of her smiling likeness for its logo, I put it on the moment it arrived and didn't take it off for my entire binge period.

But probably the most thoughtful gift came from—who else?—Oprah Winfrey. It was as if she'd seen me in Rosie's sweats and knew my depression had me eating for fifteen. Oprah's care package included several low-fat dinners pre-pared by her personal chef and flash-frozen for my dining pleasure, a basket of fruit and other low-fat snacks, two motivational audiotapes made especially for me by Oprah's Life Coaching guru, Dr. Phil, and, as if that weren't enough, a copy of every book she had ever recommended for

"Oprah's Book Club." "Let's talk," her note said simply. A handwritten P.S. provided her phone number.

I was deeply touched. But at that particular moment, I had no intention of granting interviews or appearing on anyone's TV show, not even my new pal Oprah's. My immediate objective was to ease the pain and embarrassment of the televised breakup by gorging my way into oblivion. And, just to be certain this strategy succeeded in defeating any hope of reinvigorating my social life, I had defiantly draped my rapidly expanding body in my Rosie sweats and foresworn civilized standards of personal hygiene.

My other best friend, perky Lois Torno (affectionately dubbed "the White Tornado" years ago by Norma), stopped by around six to try to cheer me up on her way to yet another soft-money fund-raiser she'd helped organize for the Democrats. Lois, who roomed with Norma and me all through Barnard, was always being stopped on the street for her uncanny resemblance to Jennifer Grey in *Dirty Dancing*, before the bad nose job. She couldn't care less about politics. But no dope, Lois had discovered a few years ago that hitting up rich donors for campaigns was a great way to meet eligible, or at least semi-eligible men of means. She'd hitched her welcome wagon to the Democrats, figuring the more socially progressive Dems would be less likely to be frightened off by her two failed marriages (no children, thank goodness). Lois claimed that at one of her political soirees last year, she was propositioned by President Clinton but turned down his invitation to "do it" on *Air Force One*. I believe the first part, but I've known Lois too long to believe the second.

Lois, the lucky girl, doesn't have to hold down a real, paying job because a few years back, Husband Number Two handed her a bundle in exchange for her agreeing to seek an annulment from the Vatican on the hazy grounds that their marriage was a case of mistaken identity. The annulment was granted, which makes you wonder how the Pope got to be Pope given that he believed the tripe Lois served up to erase the union from whatever official scorebook it is they keep in Rome. In any event, the annulment allowed the son of a bitch—the husband, not the Pope—to drop Lois for an MIT-trained programming expert at his fabulously successful dot.com company without breaking the heart of his eighty-three-year-old Italian mama, who adored Lois and taught my friend, a descendant of the only Italian mother who can't boil pasta, how to make great lasagna.

I should probably add that political fund-raising is but the latest creative strategy Lois has deployed in her never-ending quest to meet guys. I remember back in our junior year, she joined a knitting class at the 92nd Street Y to cultivate a softer image that might be more appealing to men than that of a Seven Sisters intellectual. Much to her credit, however, Lois quit in the middle of the second class when the woman seated next to her went into serious math panic counting stitches. She's man crazy, but she's no bimbo.

"What's going on?" asked Lois, eyeing my incredible haul

for the day, which was now lined up along the walls of my vestibule, piled on my large oak dining table, and distributed to numerous sites around the living room, transforming my humdrum quarters into a festive explosion of multicolored cellophane wrapping. But the first thing that struck her was that Neil's horrendous dental chair was gone. "You didn't lose a man, Marcy," she commented, "you lost an eyesore."

"Apple?" I said, offering her an impressively polished McIntosh from Oprah's basket of goodies. "It's organic. Oprah sent it."

"Right, your friend Oprah."

I handed her the card. "See for yourself."

"This is crazy," she said.

"You don't know the half of it," I said. "Barbara Walters, Diane Sawyer, and Brokaw also sent stuff. And please, let's not forget Geraldo's boxing glove."

"It's a nice color for the room," Lois commented, fingering the glove's soft red leather and then returning it to the center of the coffee table by the sofa, where I'd previously placed it as a conversation piece. "Very thoughtful."

"And Charlie Rose sent this tote," I said, lifting his canvas offering from its nearby resting place on the rug, and taking its full measure. "It looks cheap," I told Lois, "but in fairness, it's Public Television. After last night, suddenly everyone wants me to be on their show. In show-biz lingo, I'm hot. You know Mrs. Schwartz downstairs? The one whose dog has a bad bladder problem? She caught me coming in last night and asked for my autograph."

"Impressive. I guess that means Norma and I will have to stop claiming Neil never gave you anything—apart from that cheap ring and those tacky spritzers, I mean," Lois said before turning serious. "It's your due, Marcy, after all your time with that schmuck. Enjoy the ride. Which will it be, Diane or Barbara?"

"Neither," I said, matter-of-factly.

"Geraldo would be a gas," Norma continued, ignoring my response. "I hear he may be dating again. Maybe you could introduce us. I bet he'd love to go out with a gorgeous, independently wealthy Mediterranean with a fabulous body. Also a fabulous mind, of course."

"Stop showing off, Lois," I kidded back, and then pointed at her slinky black dress. "It's a Lawrence Steele, right? I saw it in *Vogue* and thought for two thousand dollars, he should throw in a little more fabric on top. It's so low-cut your boobs could fall out. Then again, I suppose nothing's too good for the Democrats."

"Very funny, Marcy. Now I'll be self-conscious."

"And, Lois, who did your hair? It looks great."

"Your Giovanni, of course. Adding the subtle blond streaks was his idea. Also putting it up. He said it would make me look in my twenties."

"Maybe even younger," I replied, still bitter over his broken promise to accentuate my cheekbones. "What did you have to do to get him to stop yapping on the cell phone and pay attention, sleep with him?"

"Well, you're in some great mood I see," Lois replied. "I

don't take it personally. But you know in your heart I'm right about the TV offers. You'd be a fool to blow them off. I'm sure Norma will tell you the same thing."

Lois picked out a large green grape from Oprah's fruit basket and placed it in her mouth, careful not to touch her meticulously applied red lip gloss. As she slowly chewed it, she looked me over. "I can't believe the hideous getup you're in," she said after a swallow. "I'll be in charge of your wardrobe and makeup."

"I'm not doing any shows," I announced. "This may come as a shock, Lois, but I don't want to make a career of being America's most famous and pathetic dumpee, even if it's only a short career, which I'm sure it would be. And for your information, Rosie sent this outfit. I like it."

"Don't get all insulted, sweetie," Lois said, reclaiming the elegant black beaded evening bag she'd nonchalantly tossed on a chair while checking out my loot. "I have nothing against Rosie. All I'm saying is, you should do her show, and some of the others, too. Live it up. Find yourself an agent who can pocket you some endorsement money before this all disappears. Neil would die seeing you on TV being treated like a star."

Lois plucked another grape from Oprah's fruit offering. "And what's this drivel about you being 'pathetic'?" she continued after consuming it. "Have you forgotten Episode Twenty? The famous one where Marcia gets braces?"

I knew immediately where she was heading. Lois was slipping back into our old *Brady Bunch* mode. Back in college, the two of us spent endless fun hours debating the deeper meaning of *Brady* plot lines, and trying to decide which of the 116 half-hour episodes most fit whatever pressing dilemma we found ourselves facing—the underlying assumption being, of course, that the show's five seasons of inane stories, dialogue, and costumes pretty thoroughly encompassed Life in all of its many complicated variations. This little game used to drive Norma nuts, not just because to her the show epitomized the worst of mass culture, or because Lois and I should have been studying, but because she suspected that to some indefinable degree, we weren't joking.

Come to think of it, Norma's distaste for *The Brady Bunch* and its supposed effect on me wasn't that much different from my mother's, except, unlike Mom, Norma never tried to bolster her case by talking up the comparative virtues of *The Lucy Show*.

"The braces episode," Lois prodded when I didn't answer immediately. "It's quintessential *Brady*, to use a favorite Q word I learned for the SATs."

"Yeah, it's a quintessential episode," I agreed. "But I'm not sure I'm up for the Bradys today. They're too upbeat. Besides, I fail to see how rehashing Marcia's orthodontic problem is supposed to help me forget my jerky orthodontist boyfriend. After last night, I'm taking a mental-health break from all things orthodontic. The way I'm feeling right now, I may even boycott my next dental cleaning."

"Marcy, think about it," Lois insisted. "You're saying

you're too pathetic to go on TV is exactly the same as Marcia Brady obsessing that her braces made her too ugly to keep her date for the school dance. Remember the ending? Her date turned out to have braces, too. So you see, she didn't have to worry. She wound up going to the dance and having a great time. Just like you should. Anyway, you can't sit home ad infinitum."

"Lois, it's been less than twenty-four hours," I said. "I have no immediate plans to leave this apartment, but to say 'ad infinitum' is a tad premature, don't you think?"

"I know just the thing," she said. "Why don't you get out of those yucky duds and come with me? Maybe we can find you a rich Democrat."

"Thanks, Lois. But if I go out, I'll just be followed by swarms of reporters and photographers. It will be exactly like Monica. I won't be able to enjoy the hors d'oeuvres in peace. They'll catch me reaching for a pig in a blanket and the next day's tabloids will be full of unflattering snapshots with captions playing off the word 'pig,' and lots of expert speculation about the amount of calories I consumed, and whether the breakup with Neil, the creep, is sapping my dietary willpower, which I can tell you with confidence, it surely is." To emphasize the point, I picked up a Godiva chocolate from Bryant Gumbel's box and tossed it into my wide-open mouth. "My current plan is to lie low for a while. I'll let you know if it changes."

"Marcy, your turning down Oprah and all the rest is either the most noble thing I've ever heard, or the most self-destructive," Lois said, giving me a quick hug as she headed out the door. "I don't have time right now to figure out which. I'm supposed to be at the event early to greet arriving VIPs. There's a cute state senator coming in from Oswego who looks promising. Call you later."

Lois did call later. The state senator from Oswego, she reported, turned out to be gay.

"I didn't know they allowed gay people in upstate New York," I said. "But maybe that explains why he left upstate to come to the party."

"Not funny, Marcy," Lois said. "Man-wise, the night was a bust. The good news is, I have at least one friend who's not above giving TV interviews. I forgot to tell you. Norma's on Ted Koppel tonight to plug her new book."

Ted Koppel. Good for him, I thought, and not for having the foresight to book Norma Ruckenhaus, well-known feminist intellectual. I was thinking instead of the notable absence of the host of *Nightline* among the media biggies plying me with flowers and candy to get me to bare my soul, such as it is, on their program.

Flipping the channels to find Norma, my timing coincided with the end of the local news shows. Lucky me. I landed on channel 5 just as Liz Smith was launching into a review of my humiliating introduction to the viewing public, reading text off the TelePrompTer I gathered she was recycling from her syndicated column. "It was a long, rough night for Marcy Lee Mallowitz, but I confess I enjoyed every minute," gushed the veteran gossip czarina, her tone unduly chipper, I thought, considering it was my life she was talking about. "Like a lot of what transpires these days under the nouvelle heading of 'reality TV,' Marcy's blowup with her beau on *Filthy Rich!* was at once tasteless and transfixing—sort of like munching popcorn at a train wreck."

I then had the eerie experience of watching different stations play the same humiliating video clip of the previous night's *Filthy Rich!* fracas. Fortunately, I had the foresight to put the sound on mute, so I was able to avoid any snide remarks by the blow-dried anchors.

The part they kept playing is where Neil calls me a bitch, starts screaming *"Comedy Hour, Comedy Hour, Comedy Hour,"* and I respond by yelling back and throwing the ring. In the playback, Neil seemed even angrier than I remembered, his body language even more menacing. Also, I had to give my mother credit. I looked pretty good in that Saks number we picked out for the show. Even on sale, it cost a lot of dead roaches, as my dad would say. But they were dead roaches well spent.

After playing the clip, channel 9 announced the results of a brand-new poll. Americans, according to the survey, were so impressed by the way I stood up to Neil that they now rated me among the world's most admired women—behind Eleanor Roosevelt and Mother Teresa, to be sure, but before another woman with man problems, Hillary Clinton. Don't get a swelled head, I told myself. A week from now, probably only a few die-hard *Filthy Rich!* fans will remember your name. Adding insult, I thought, by then I'll probably be replaced on the list by the latest contestant to be ejected from the phony island paradise where they shoot *The Plank*.

The Plank, I needn't tell you, is the hot new "reality show," which at that moment was threatening to equal, or even surpass, the phenomenal success of *Filthy Rich!*, notwithstanding its cheesy production values and a ludicrous format that lends credence to my theory that someone—perhaps visiting Russian spies piqued by the long lines at Disneyland—has slipped a mild hallucinogenic into the bottled water consumed by the TV big shots charged with deciding which programs America gets to see. Each week on the *The Plank*, in case you haven't seen it, network executives dressed in elaborate pirate costumes drive around environmentally sensitive beach areas in flashy BMW convertibles, sometimes getting stuck in the sand. But the real drama comes at the end of the hour when the "pirates" capture the scantily clad contestant who registered the lowest likability with viewers in the Q rating the week before, and force him or her to walk a specially constructed plank to an awaiting rowboat, thereby tossing the person off the island and the show. The plank is decorated with the show's logo of a winking pirate done in blue-and-gold glitter, so it stands out in the aerial shots that open and close the program.

Although it looks like all this action is taking place on a remote tropical island, *The Plank* is actually filmed on a back lot in Burbank. The rats and bugs the pirates/executives devour in dining scenes are actually filet mignon, unless, of course, they requested chicken a few days in advance to help keep down their cholesterol. To maintain the show's authenticity, the contestants are fed real rats and bugs.

I tried to watch *The Plank* once to see what all the hoopla was about on a night my worthless former roomie was working late—catching up on making molds of patients' teeth, he said. I was deep in snoozeland after about ten minutes, and I wasn't even tired. I just couldn't stand the tedium anymore, and I was too lazy to get up from the sofa to search for the remote, which Neil, the scuzzy piece of dentifrice, had stored somewhere without informing me of the location for about the trillionth time. The only thing more distasteful than the show itself, in my book (other than Neil), is the mean-spirited Miller Lite commercial, where a half dozen professional football players chase a short, chubby, bearded guy out of a bar yelling, "Go back to the island, weirdo," when they figure out he's Brad Thatcher, the cunning cross-dressing plumber from outside Hartford who, by virtue of his victory in *The Plank*'s first survival test, is now a world-famous celebrity. I fail to see the humor in any kind of bigotry, although I surmise that Thatcher is laughing all the way to the bank.

The last thing I remember before dozing off for the night was hearing Norma accuse the nation's leading male fashion designers of a conscious plot to subjugate women by raising hemlines.

"Ted," she said, trying to stir controversy and book sales, "we're talking about men who want to exploit women, but don't really like them. I ask: Why else expose their knees?"

I thought Norma made a good point. It's a lot harder to take someone seriously around the office if her skirt crawls up to her gizzard each time she sits down. But the ever-sensible moderator wasn't buying my friend's antifeminist conspiracy theory. "Come now, Ms. Ruckenhaus," Koppel said, "surely there's more to fashion than a desire to keep women down. I daresay Calvin Klein and the others have prospered precisely because women are more liberated, not the other way around. And pardon me for saying this, but I detect a tinge of sexism in your implicit assumption that women will go along like sheep with whatever these gentlemen say is fashion. And what about the female designers? I don't see them complaining."

Koppel promised Norma a chance to respond after a commercial break. But by then, I was already fast asleep, dreaming I was being chased by a giant toothbrush.

A recurring comedy sketch on what popular show featured a character, Laverne, sharing dirt about men with her friend at the Laundromat?

a. *The Sonny and Cher Comedy Hour*
b. *The Joan Rivers Show*
c. *The Carol Burnett Show*
d. *Saturday Night Live*

See correct answer on back. . . .

Seven

✦

Oops. In the depressing aftermath of my network television debut, and distracted by the likes of Barbara Walters wooing me for a tell-all chat, I'd forgotten all about my clients. My subconscious sent me a flash about this dereliction of duty around 6 A.M., causing me to awake with a start.

I felt truly awful, and not just because I'm the sort of gal who deeply resents rising with the roosters. Barely thirty-six hours ago, in a pitifully public trauma, I'd lost the man I thought I was going to marry. Now, it seemed, I was on a fast track to pissing away my fulfilling career as the Personal Life Coach to a churning assemblage of striving, well-to-do ladies.

I thought of poor Dolores Smithers, the forty-three-year-old financial wizard, whose scheduled two o'clock session the previous afternoon had completely slipped my mind. Dolores, having already banked a small fortune, no longer saw her future in pork bellies. Instead, she was counting on my coaching assistance to realize her long-standing dream of becoming the proud proprietor/artistic director of a crafts shop specializing in delicate macramé items with a nautical motif. Yesterday, I recalled glumly, we were supposed to go to a big yarn store together. I hoped that my no-show wouldn't dampen her resolve to make the break from the pressured job and lifestyle she had grown to hate.

By the way, the field trip to the yarn store is an example of a useful technique I call "strategic realization." Getting Dolores to see and smell the wool she yearned to commune with on a full-time basis would, I felt, move her a critical step closer to finding the courage to pursue her true passion in the wonderful world of macramé miniatures. It took seven hour-long sessions to persuade Dolores to take an afternoon off from work to make the woolly journey. Now, I feared, it would probably take seven more just to persuade her not to fire me and find a new Personal Life Coach.

I played back my messages. There was one from my mother, natch, this time to announce that if she didn't hear from me in an hour she was assuming I didn't mind her giving *People* magazine some "nice" pictures of her newly (in)famous daughter.

"Can you imagine, Marcy," Mom said, "you're going to be in *People*. The neighbors are so excited they practically have *shpilkes*."

"*Shpilkes*" is a great Yiddish word meaning "ants in your pants." I didn't know about the neighbors, but the idea of my mother blathering about my private life to a reporter from *People* was enough to give me a serious case.

"The reporter asked about you and Neil," continued her message. "I told her I never liked him. He's an orthodontist who won't treat children, for God's sake. What kind of father is that for my grandchildren?"

Good work, Mom, I thought. That will teach me not to answer my phone or message machine in a timely manner. The Marcy Lee Mallowitz story was now going to get the *People* treatment whether I wanted it or not. I just hoped my mother would have the good sense not to share my baby bath photos or, even worse, high school prom pictures of me wearing big, teased hair the friendly trainee at the local beauty shop managed to elevate by spraying tons of sticky hair spray that kept me sneezing all night, with my dorky date, Eugene from next door, at my side. Not to dwell on the excessive hair spray, but I'm certain scientists one day will confirm that the reduction in the ozone layer caused by my prom preparations is the real reason for global warming.

Before Mom could hang up, my dad grabbed the phone to remind me, much as he always did when I was going through a rough spot, that I was still his "favorite," and that the job offer with the family exterminating company still stood. "You say aquamarine trucks, Marcy, we'll do aquamarine," he signed off. "But will you think about navy? It hides the dirt." By now this was a set routine, not unlike Dad's dead-roach count. But it always made me smile.

His message was followed by one from my friend Lois. She had concocted a creative scheme for me to meet "smart, sensitive guys," and couldn't wait to share it. "We'll enroll you in the 'Holocaust Studies' course for adult singles at the Ethical Culture Society," she said. "*New York* magazine this week calls it 'the hip, new Dating Central.' Call back right away. Maybe I'll do it with you."

Crazy Lois, I thought. After all those rubber-chicken dinners with Democratic fat cats, I think she's finally lost it. I wasn't going to use Hitler to meet a new man, even if the price of the course did include complimentary free drinks. I was not that desperate. Yet.

In addition to Mom, Dad, and Lois, and follow-up calls from the gift-bearing media bigs, there was a long message from NBC's Tim Russert. He apologized for not sending anything (he pleaded that he'd been "out of town") and invited me to appear on a special segment of *Meet the Press*, which, of course, he moderates.

I had the strangest reaction. Instead of being flattered by Russert's attention, or offended by the relaxation of standards that led him to think I was *Meet the Press* worthy, I felt mildly insulted by his delay in contacting me, not to mention his lame excuse—"I was out of town." Yeah, right. Hadn't he ever heard of Harry & David? And HELLO THERE, what about 1-800-Flowers? This is the new millennium. You don't have to be in town to send a fruit basket or a nourishing gift box of Terra chips with assorted salsas. I made a mental note that if I ever did decide to break my public silence, it would not be on *Meet the Press*.

Farewell to the old, self-aware Marcy Mallowitz who only the night before was mentally praising Ted Koppel for ignoring her. Literally overnight, a new, not necessarily improved Marcy began to emerge—call her "Marcy, the Media Babe." I was still lying low at home in my comfy pink sweatsuit from Rosie O'Donnell. But there was no disguising my change in outlook. Where at first I saw all of the gifts and attention coming my way as a humiliating reminder of Neil's dumping me on *Filthy Rich!*—a pretty sad claim to fame when you think about it—I now viewed them as an entitlement. It's an unattractive transformation but one that's hard to avoid. Just ask the two former Mrs. Donald Trumps, Marla and Ivana, or for that matter any of those much-sought-after rejects from *The Plank*.

Beyond my mother, Lois, and Tim Russert, the tape also contained a pile of messages from publishing houses and advertising honchos wanting to explore various commercial opportunities that might prove mutually beneficial. The most remunerative, though not necessarily the most appealing, was an offer to become the official spokeswoman for that exciting dietary breakthrough, kosher Baco Bits. I was honored by my selection, of course, and thought the exceptional minds who run this prestige outfit made a savvy choice. But that didn't mean I intended to return the call. Or any of the other calls. I was a Personal Life Coach. More accurately, by that point, I suppose, a Personal Life Coach with Attitude. In any case, I still had no intention of bootstrapping my one catastrophic appearance on *Filthy Rich!* into drive-by guest gigs on *Meet the Press* and tons of shows lower on the food chain. Nor did I intend to exploit my accidental turn in the spotlight by pitching sacrilegious food products meant to enhance the salad-eating experience.

Oh, I almost forgot. There was also a message from Dolores. I must be blocking because at the time it was a very big deal. Instead of expressing anger at my standing her up at the yarn store, she sounded sympathetic. She said she "totally understood," given how upset I must be. She also said I could call her any hour of the day if I wanted to talk to her about "the things that were troubling" me. She even suggested that I hop on an exercise bike and ride ten miles to reduce my stress and "restore that sense of calm equilibrium everybody needs to function properly."

Hey, I thought, I'm the Personal Life Coach. She's supposed to be the client. But thanks to the blowup on *Filthy Rich!* our roles were now reversed. Dolores was trying to coach me, using the same reliable lines of wisdom and encouragement I'd used on her maybe hundreds of times over.

I had to face facts. You can't be an effective Personal Life Coach when your own life is so visibly pathetic that even your highly self-absorbed clients are moved to focus on some other person's problems, not their own—and *you* are that other person. The distance and respect that are prerequisites for my profession were gone, just as good old Neil was gone.

Uh-oh, I said to myself, struggling not very successfully to fend off the sad feelings starting to wash over me, along with an overpowering, and not altogether pleasant, sense of déjà vu. For the second time in my life, I was entering the dicey economic and emotional terrain I call "Gap Country": a period of professional uncertainty and turmoil that finds you clinging for comfort to the notion that if your career doesn't start looking up, and soon, you could always find work at a nearby Gap clothing store. Indeed, the very ubiquity of the Gap's outlets for vending its strangely appealing generic preppy wear, which just yesterday you condemned as urban blight, suddenly becomes your major source of security and hope.

My first experience in this scary realm dates back nearly eight years. I had just left Santa Monica Spaces, and it wasn't yet clear whether I'd succeed in building a sufficiently large roster of well-paying clients to make a successful transition from closet consulting to my newly chosen profession of Personal Life Coach. The one thing that *was* certain from my standpoint was that I wasn't going to go back to closets, or back to Brooklyn to take up the giant bug sprayer my sweet dad kept calling to say he had all filled and waiting for me. Becoming a Gap employee, or "Gapster," as I prefer to call this exclusive club, was at least something different. On the bright side, moreover, it wasn't lost on me that directing inquiring Gap customers to the location of the store's sales racks can be considered *a helping profession*, in its way.

There were nearly two months when practically every waking hour I wasn't seeing my few existing clients, or massaging the contacts I hoped would lead to new ones, was spent skulking amid the meticulously stacked piles of new clothing displayed on the selling floor of the Gap store nearest my home, boning up just in case. Originally I worried that my mediocre folding skills, which I never found to be a real impediment in redesigning people's closets, might disqualify me for a job whose central responsibility involves arranging garments into incredibly neat stacks. But that was before I learned the secret behind the Gap's superhuman stacking. That secret is the utilization of ingenious plastic forms, which make precision folding pretty foolproof even for people like me whose attempts to master hospital corners have always ended in humiliation. The feeling of relief when I spotted a young female employee casually using such a form to straighten a pile of children's sweaters one night just before closing is indescribable.

Recalling that sweet moment of revelation somehow supplied me with the courage to confront what needed doing if I were to have any chance of preserving my hard-won Life Coaching career. Yes, Marcy, I thought, in a pinch there's always the Gap.

At precisely 9 A.M., still wearing Rosie's sweatsuit and munching one of the talk-show queen's Twinkies for breakfast, I began dialing my clients, including Dolores, to cancel all appointments for the next few weeks. By then, I figured, wiping away a tiny dollop of white Twinkie cream that had fallen onto the pink sweatshirt, either something good would happen to put my life back on track again, or my clients, who have a notably short attention span when it comes to *other* folks' problems, would forget that their Life Coach was such a well-known mess.

I was waiting for the message tape to rewind, wondering how I was going to finance my self-imposed layoff, when my doorman Frank arrived with yet more floral and candy bribes from Leeza, Queen Latifah, and the gang. Easily the day's most unusual offering came from Marcia Clark, the ex-assistant Los Angeles district attorney who parlayed her bungling of O. J. Simpson's prosecution into a $4.2 million book deal, an image-enhancing beauty makeover, and a glitzy new career as a TV legal commentator and talk-show host: a pair of fine leather gloves from Bergdorf's that recalled the most famous piece of evidence from the televised trial that launched her as a celebrity. Except for the absence of blood, of course. "I'll be subbing for Geraldo next week," she wrote on the card. "Would love you as a guest."

The fresh supply of expensive loot confirmed that memories of my *Filthy Rich!* appearance had yet to fade.

Through no fault of my own, I'd become the starring player in a made-for-television melodrama whose ending was not yet in sight. Americans were still standing around office watercoolers and in supermarket checkout lines debating whether it's ever okay to serve as your boyfriend's Lifeline, and whether I acted hastily in tossing the ring at Neil instead of trying to patch things up by docilely apologizing for my costly confusion over Teri Garr's curriculum vitae. In other words, celebrity, if I really wanted it, was still out there waiting for me.

When I tried to put everything in perspective—and apart from snacking and thinking about the Gap, it was mostly what I did—I just got more confused. Whoopi Goldberg was offering me my own box on *Hollywood Squares*. I was perfectly aware I'd done nothing to earn the honor other than to make a dangerous projectile of Neil's crummy ring. But like I've said, I was getting less humble by the minute. I was feeling entitled. Hell, I figured, why shouldn't Whoopi invite me? I can be more entertaining than Jim Nabors.

Yet that swagger notwithstanding, the odds that I would actually say yes to assuming one of the august squares remained slim, and not just because I wanted to avoid having to list "square" as my profession on the next Barnard alumnae questionnaire. Unlike Lucy Ricardo and most everyone else I know, I never really had show-biz aspirations. If you check out the high school play program my mother has squirreled away in her extensive Marcy Memorabilia Collection, you'll see that my only real entertainment credit prior to Neil Night on *Filthy Rich!* was a small footnote thanking me and about ten other students listed in alphabetical order for our help painting sets for the junior-class production of *Storybook Theater*. Avidly following the travails of my favorite celebrities in the gossip pages, as I have for years, has provided me with a daily dose of vicarious excitement and glamour, but without instilling any real ambition to become one myself.

Moreover, there was the not-so-little matter of taste. I cringed at the thought that I—Marcy Lee Mallowitz—

risked becoming forever identified as a prime example of
the habitual elevation of unaccomplished nobodies a recent
cover story in *Newsweek* dubbed "America's Growing
Pseudo-Celebrity Crisis." I don't disagree that there is such
a crisis or that so-called reality shows like *Filthy Rich!* and
The Plank are its epicenter. Only please do me a favor and
keep my good name out of it.

Thus my decision to stay holed up in my apartment,
dressed in yesterday's sweats and popping fancy chocolates,
was not part of some carefully calculated strategy to
heighten the media's interest in yours truly. But it seemed
to have that effect, turning me into some sort of game show
Greta Garbo.

Speaking of the ring, it wasn't long after Frank brought up
the gifts that he made a return trip, this time bearing a note
hand-delivered by a man Frank described under my interro-
gation as a "tall, decent-looking sort, probably fortyish."

"Dear Ms. Mallowitz," said the note, which was typed on
plain white paper, "You don't know me, but I was at the
show, and think your ex-boyfriend is a real jerk. I saw that
junky ring he gave you sitting on the floor of the set as
everyone was leaving, and I took the liberty of grabbing it
and selling it for you on eBay. It went yesterday for $5,200.
I have the check, and if you have a moment, I'd like to
deliver it in person." The letter was signed, "Your fan, Cliff
Jentzen."

I was touched that someone—a perfect stranger—would
go to the trouble of selling the ring for me. I was also

impressed by the financial result. Hey, I thought to myself, $5,200 is probably $5,000 more than Neil paid for it. Amazing thing, the power of television.

"He's in the lobby, waiting," Frank said. "I told him I could give you the check, but he said he'd rather wait and do it himself."

"You left him alone there in the lobby?" I asked Frank.

"Yeah, he seems like a nice enough guy," Frank said. "Decent-looking. I don't think he's the type to steal Social Security checks from the mailboxes when no one's looking. No harm in you saying hello. I could send him up if you want."

"Frank," I said, "not so fast. We don't know anything about this mystery benefactor of mine. Maybe he's from the *National Enquirer*, and the eBay bit is just a ruse to get an interview or a photo of me looking like a slob. Or, he could be a more conventional weirdo who saw me on TV and developed a sick obsession. Or maybe he just wants to worm a big tip out of me. I can't say he doesn't deserve it. And then, of course, there's always the possibility that this Cliff Jentzen, if that's his real name, is as nice as you say."

"Maybe," Frank said. He was now my co-conspirator. If I met this guy in the lobby, the two of us strategized, I would be sacrificing any expectation of privacy, as a handful of reporters and lensmen were still camped outside the building hungry for breaking developments in the Marcy Lee Mallowitz story. I could also be sacrificing a lot of money, since once informed of the ring's fate, Neil, the cheapskate, was certain to insist on being cut in. Knowing Neil, he would probably demand the whole wad. So my doorman and I devised Plan Two: I would meet this Jentzen fellow in the basement laundry room. The place has security cameras up the wazoo, we figured, so Frank would be able to keep an eye on things from the monitors in the lobby.

"If he's bad news, I'll signal for you to come running," I said. "Just promise me, Frank, you won't leave on a coffee break."

We shook on it.

"Okay, then," I said. "The laundry room in five minutes."

Within seconds of laying that plan, the stomach butterflies from the other night came fluttering back with a vengeance. As I rode the elevator down to the basement, I felt as jittery as Marcia Brady at the very beginning of Episode Seventy-five. It was very perplexing. Marcia had good reason to be nervous: She was facing her first day of high school. What was my excuse?

The elevator doors opened, landing me in the middle of the musty basement storage area. On the left, just before the door to the laundry room, I was surprised to see Neil's ugly black-leather "thinking chair." He'd apparently parked it there for safekeeping on his hurried way out the door the other night. It had a white piece of paper Scotch-taped to the seat with his name on it, and a notation: "Save for Pickup." On it, someone in the building—I assumed it was my doorman Frank—had scrawled "Good riddance, you bastard" in red Flair pen, and signed it with a reasonable approximation of a skull and crossbones.

I had a good mind to remove the note and ask this Jentzen guy with whom I was about to rendezvous to try making another sale for me on eBay.

What was the name of the restaurant opened by Jack Tripper on *Three's Company*?

a. The Galloping Gourmet
b. Jack's Eatery
c. The Regal Beagle
d. Jack's Bistro

See correct answer on back. . . .

Eight

◆

Quick, give me a five-letter word meaning "Dumped Female Lifeline."

The answer, of course, is M-A-R-C-Y. Yes, me. Marcy Lee Mallowitz. If you got that right, give yourself a generous pat on the back; you've clearly been paying close attention. Moreover, you've correctly completed number 8 Down in *The New York Times* crossword puzzle that appeared the same day my mystery eBay hero turned up out of the blue. Lucky for me, I was unaware of this mocking reference at the time, as I probably would have been too depressed to leave my apartment and go meet him. I was feeling plenty down already without any crossword *tsoris*.

On a more philosophical, less purely egotistical level, my mention in the crossword amounted to jarring confirmation that my television travails had already become part of the cultural vocabulary. Much as I tried to resist, I was nevertheless getting thrust into Darvaland. Any day now, I expect to see an erudite *New Yorker* essay by Daniel Patrick

Moynihan expounding on my unwarranted emergence in the spotlight—"Defining Celebrity Down." Personally, I'm not sufficiently deep or insightful enough to know exactly what my rise to fame on the flimsy basis of one brief, embarrassing appearance on *Filthy Rich!* says about our society, me, or the clever wordsmiths who write the *Times* crossword. But I have a sinking feeling it isn't good.

There is something strangely comforting about watching someone else's laundry sloshing about in a sea of suds through the round glass window of a communal washing machine. You can enjoy the rhythm of the waves without worrying if those stain-zapping enzymes used to fortify Extra-Strength Tide with Bleach are dissolving the giant ketchup stain threatening to force your favorite blouse into retirement. At least that's what I was thinking as I waited for my male visitor amid the half dozen coin machines in the basement of my building. This may be idiosyncratic on my part, but the spin cycle, I have found, can be almost hypnotic.

Just as I was nearing a trancelike state, I heard a man's deep voice. "Marcy, Marcy Mallowitz, that you?"

Startled, I turned around.

"Cliff Jentzen," the man said. "Sorry if I scared you."

On quick inspection, he looked to be fortyish and quite "decent-looking," much as my doorman Frank had described. He was clad in a worn pair of jeans with a subtle blue-plaid cotton shirt I was almost sure came from J. Crew.

A slight paunch suggested exercise deprivation, but nothing a month's worth of gym visits couldn't significantly reverse. Between his friendly manner, cute cleft chin, and full head of slightly disheveled wavy brown hair, the overall vibes were positive. Make that *very* positive.

"Hi," I said as we rather tentatively shook hands. "Welcome to my private office." I withdrew my hand somewhat quickly, preferring to risk appearing a tad impolite than make a permanent bad impression with my sweaty palms. "It's a little noisy," I added, gesturing with my other moist hand to the surrounding machines, "but you can't beat the location if you like doing laundry as much as I do."

"I'm not real big on laundry," he said without missing a beat, "it's the decor I can't get enough of." Not a Henny Youngman classic maybe, but as throwaway banter goes, not bad. Definitely a big improvement over Neil's lame nitrous oxide jokes. In the three years I was with Neil, I couldn't recall him ever saying anything funny. Not ha-ha funny. At least not on purpose.

Whoa, Marcy, I reminded myself. This guy's here to deliver a check, not be checked out for a date. It's just two days since Neil gave you the heave-ho. What would it do to your media profile if it got out you were back on the hunt already?

That was followed by a warring message from a small, decidedly unhip corner of my brain. Whaddaya talking, "media profile"? Two days ago, you didn't even have one. Get back to business. You still don't know if Cliff Jentzen is really a guardian angel who sold Neil's junky ring on eBay for you, or some kind of reporter or even a pervert.

And, of course, one more important thought: Idiot, why are you still in your Rosie sweats?

"Well, here's the check," he said, handing over a small, folded blue piece of paper he excavated from one of the back pockets of his jeans.

I opened the check and looked it over. It was for $5,200 all right, but it was a personal check from his account, raising my suspicions.

"I'm confused," I said. "I thought the ring sold on eBay. Why your personal check?"

"Don't worry, I'll get the money back. But the eBay payment could take a few days. I thought it would make you happy to get the money now. I thought you could probably use a lift."

"You're right about that," I said, folding the check back in half and hunting for a sweatpants pocket to store it in.

Zip. Bam. End of transaction, I figured.

Happily, I was wrong.

"Much as I love laundry rooms," Cliff said, "how about continuing this conversation elsewhere—say, lunch?"

"Lunch?" I said dumbly, as if totally unfamiliar with the concept of a midday meal.

"Yeah, lunch," he said. "It's almost noon, and giving away big checks makes me hungry. How about it?"

The only trouble, I explained, was that I hadn't been outside once since the show. I wanted things to die down. "This publicity stuff is not my thing," I said.

"I gather," he said. "And I think it's great the way you're holding out. The media sharks circling around you don't deserve the time of day. The kind of fame they're peddling is a pile of crap, as far as I'm concerned. Real life is too important to sell out to ratings and reality TV. On the other hand, just because your ex-boyfriend makes a fool of himself in front of the whole country is no reason your life should totally stop. He's the one who should feel embarrassed."

"Thanks for that positive spin. Everyone else is saying I'm nuts not to go for the gold. I'm a little confused at this point."

"That's just your body saying you need fresh air," he said. "I know the press can be pesky, so I brought this just in case." He pulled a wrinkled, deep-purple bandanna from his back pants pocket and waved it like a flag. "Ta-da."

Instantly, I thought of my Life Coaching client Jane McDee, the hamburger heiress with the bad dye job and the buck teeth it seemed Neil had been working on forever. She had a lot of bandannas in her collection, but not this particular shade of purple.

"Put it on," Cliff instructed, handing me the bandanna. "We'll add my sunglasses, and you'll just look like another weird New Yorker."

He had our escape planned. "We can slip out the building's service exit, and no one will know you're gone. My car's parked right outside. I know a great Chinese place in

Astoria. It's a real melting-pot neighborhood—full of new immigrants who speak every conceivable language except English. Barbara Walters and her friends will never find you. Promise."

The invitation was even more irresistible than the baskets of fattening edibles upstairs. "It's worth a try," I said, tying on the scarf.

Just as we were departing the laundry room, my door-man Frank appeared. I'd forgotten he was watching our meeting unfold on the lobby's security monitors. This provoked an instantaneous flicker of recognition. Just like contestants on that sick shiver-me-timbers show, *The Plank*, forget about the cameras watching their every move, I realized.

"That you, Ms. Mallowitz?" Frank said, plainly puzzled by the bandanna and dark Ray-Bans I was sporting. "Everything okay?"

"Fine, Frank," I said. "Everything is fine."

I know what you're thinking. Her judgment sucks. Has she never heard the phrase "decent interval"? Besides, she got the same positive vibes when she first met Neil, and look what a self-centered meanie he turned out to be. She doesn't even know yet what the man does for a living, and she's getting in an automobile with him to go eat Chinese in some colorful ethnic neighborhood in Queens? That's not lunch. That's a DATE!

We think alike. These same thoughts occurred to me as I was trying to scrunch into the front seat of his '91 Corolla without cracking any of the plastic disc boxes messily lining the floor. Given my background, I recoiled at this clue of what his closets at home must look like. A momentary panic set in. But then I said to myself: Marcy Lee, you knew from the start that Neil was a great orthodontist, and very neat, and where did that get you? Insulted and abandoned on prime-time network television three years later, that's where.

I know my track record in the man department does not inspire confidence. But trust me on this one. Besides, as I kept trying to reassure myself during the half-hour ride to Astoria: This wasn't a date. We were just having lunch.

A long lunch, as it turned out.

The restaurant was a small, unpretentious jewel only recently discovered by *Zagat*. We arrived a little after twelve-thirty and stayed until around four, by which time some of the other tables were occupied by seniors there to take advantage of the early-bird dinner specials.

Here is what I found out about my companion, apart from his weakness for extra-spicy Kung Pao Chicken. Cliff was raised in Plainview, Long Island, which I wouldn't have guessed, since he retained as little of his Long Island accent as I retain of Brooklynese. He was a big sports guy in high school, which led to a track scholarship to Cornell, where he graduated (barely, he claimed) a couple of years before I finished Barnard. Since then, best as I could piece together, he'd held different jobs. Lately, he told me, he'd been working "in production," which I took to mean that he was some kind of packaged-goods middle manager. Not much glamour to it, I supposed, but a lot of free samples.

He wasn't a doctor, which would disappoint my mom. But, if we ended up going out, at least I could tell her he wasn't some out-of-work bum.

Somehow I never did find out what Cliff was doing at *Filthy Rich!* But he said it was "spunky" the way I threw the ring at Neil and gave him what for. "Unlike Lou Grant," he explained, drawing a contrast to the gruff but lovable newsroom boss on *The Mary Tyler Moore Show* that bespoke a certain sitcom savvy, "I *like* spunk. Actually, I like it a lot." He made it clear he wasn't just being a Good Samaritan picking up the ring and selling it for me; he wanted an excuse to meet me.

Oh, and this is important: Cliff said that while he had come close to marriage a couple of times, he had never tied the knot. He broke up with his last steady girlfriend, a veterinarian specializing in exotic birds, he explained, because he began to get the feeling she cared for her feathered patients more than she cared for him. Cliff said that was more than a year ago.

Mostly, however, we didn't talk about Cliff. Mostly, we talked about me, which I wasn't exactly used to after three years of Neil's steady blathering about his amazing breakthroughs in orthodontics. Cliff just kept peppering me with questions, even to the point of exploring my close but complicated relationship with my mother, which, I realized while talking it over, had become even more complicated in the aftermath of *Filthy Rich!*

For my mother, I explained, the whole idea of being in *People* was a dream come true. It's not really that she's shallow. It's just she can blot out the humiliating reason *People* was interested. She's like the rest of America, which sees celebrity as a laudable achievement in and of itself.

"So what makes you different?" Cliff wanted to know. "You obviously grew up loving television. Classic comedies at least, though not *Sonny and Cher*."

"That was a *variety show*," I reminded him. It was still a sore point. But thinking about it, my resistance to being celebritized was probably a form of delayed rebellion. I have one friend who was dragged to Loehmann's by her mother so much as a kid, she now refuses to buy anything on sale. Me, I didn't want to be famous for being dumped by my boyfriend on a game show, even if it *was* in prime time. I'd gotten some interesting offers, though. I told Cliff about the one from kosher Baco Bits.

Cliff paid the check, and I was tying on the bandanna again, getting ready to leave, when our server, a silver-haired Chinese lady who didn't speak any English, returned to the table and started waving her order pad in my face. She kept repeating something in Chinese, and the more we tried to tell her we didn't understand, the more agitated she seemed to become. Finally, her son, the restaurant's owner, came over.

"Please excuse Mother," he said. "She saw you on TV, that *Filthy Rich!* She wants your autograph."

Cliff and I looked at each other and laughed. Then, naturally, I obliged this new fan. "Best wishes," I wrote, "Marcy Lee Mallowitz." Next to my name, I drew a smiley face, something I intentionally omitted when I signed for the unlikable Mrs. Schwartz from my building. I also posed for a picture with the owner. If I ever return to the place, I thought, I fully expect to find it hanging on the wall by the tiny coatroom in the front of the restaurant, along with pictures of the governor, Senator Hillary Rodham Clinton, Tony Bennett, and the owner's other famous diners.

On *Gilligan's Island*, Jim Backus played the blustery millionaire Thurston Howell III. What was the name of his flighty society wife?

a. Muffy
b. Lovey
c. Mimsey
d. Lulu

See correct answer on back. . . .

ANSWER

✦

b. Lovey

Nine

✦

It occurs to me that I haven't told you yet about Ellewina Nash Goldberg, my all-time favorite Personal Life Coaching client. Ellewina, as readers of the society pages may already know, was the daughter of Aldous Nash, the rabid right-wing industrialist and mortal enemy of Franklin Roosevelt. Her rebellion against her family took the form of marrying a Jewish socialist from Queens, Myron Goldberg, whom she met at a Norman Thomas rally in the thirties. Their marriage, which lasted half a century and produced three daughters, all of whom live in big mansions in Greenwich, ended when Myron quite unexpectedly ran off with the nubile eighteen-year-old waitress who served him fruit cocktail at a buffet fund-raising dinner he attended with Ellewina at Donald Trump's Mar-a-Lago in Palm Beach.

Well, to say Myron "ran off" is actually something of a misnomer, as by then the cad was in the early stage of Parkinson's disease and got around using a walker. But, of course, that made the situation no less painful for poor Ellewina.

By the time Ellewina reached out to me for coaching, her father was long gone, and she herself was a widow. Myron, not long after dashing off with his young cutie, had expired from a heart attack brought on by the mysterious Chinese herbs he'd taken to boost his libido. Well into her seventies, Ellewina was hampered by poor eyesight and slowed by advancing arthritis in her joints, but was otherwise in decent health.

Moreover, unlike a lot of oldsters, Ellewina did not have to worry about money. As her father grew older, he became quite fond of Myron and put Ellewina back in his will. Indeed, near his death at the age of ninety-two, old Mr. Nash wrote a much-admired op-ed piece for *The New York Times* in which he expressed regret at his previous anti-Semitism and publicly resigned his membership in several exclusive clubs, all as a prelude to explaining his recent decision to convert to Judaism.

Anyway, Ellewina sought my help to get rid of the terrible depression she'd fallen into as a result of hanging out with people her own age.

"All they do is sit around and complain about their latest ailment," she said. "Isn't it possible anymore to have a friendly conversation where no one uses the words bowel or bladder? I can't listen anymore. I know it sounds silly at my advanced age, but I need to change my life."

My strategy was to get Ellewina actively engaged in the

various charitable causes she supported instead of simply handing the money to the New York Community Trust to dole out.

The going wasn't always smooth. There was the time, for example, when Ellewina threw a party at her vast seaside estate in Southampton to raise money for impoverished Native Americans out west. "We must help our Indians" was her mantra as she greeted each new arrival, most of whom came clad in elaborate beaded outfits, thinking the soiree was a costume party. But the event probably wouldn't have generated so much bad press had it not been for the decision to hand out fuzzy dice in authentic Native American hues as the party favor. What can I say? I was young, and just starting out in the Personal Coaching game. I take the blame, totally.

But I more than made up for that travesty by my next move. I persuaded Ellewina to endow a new charity for inner-city youth, the Groucho Foundation, she called it. She came up with that name, she told me, having read that Oprah Winfrey called her company Harpo Productions. I explained that Harpo is only Oprah spelled backward. I suggested instead the Ellewina Nash Goldberg Foundation. But there was no moving Ellewina when her mind was already made up. "Groucho was my favorite of the brothers," she said.

What matters is that the Groucho Foundation has helped a lot of kids. It also helped Ellewina by giving her a new sense of purpose, as well as a dandy excuse to eschew her crabby contemporaries and hang out with the energetic young staff members we hired for the program.

She frequently thanked me for getting her off her "lazy duff." But after those first few productive sessions together, it was never clear to me which of us was the coach, and who was being helped more. We had become friends.

One day, I accompanied Ellewina when she visited a daycare center, supported almost entirely by her foundation, in a poor section of the Bronx. By now her charitable activities had made her a well-recognized New York icon, and she always made it a point not to "dress down" when she went on one of these inspection tours, so as "not to disappoint." For this occasion, she wore a turquoise-and-gold brocade number that was elegant in an Old World sort of way, and could have passed for drapes.

The staff of the center, who greeted her like a movie star, had obviously gone to a lot of trouble to prepare a special lunch: inexpensive packaged bologna and other choice cold cuts on Wonder bread. When the platter was presented to her, I didn't know what to expect. Honestly, I wasn't sure whether she'd ever seen white bread with crust before. She could easily have declined the fare, pleading another engagement, or that she had already eaten. Instead the spunky doyenne surveyed the jars of mustard, ketchup, and mayonnaise proudly arrayed on a drab metal table, and then took a little of each before biting enthusiastically into her bologna and American cheese sandwich. "My," she said, her mouth still full of cheap processed meat, "what lovely sauces."

I remember thinking at the time, I wish I could be like Ellewina and see "lovely sauces" in crummy store-brand jars of condiments.

Ellewina died peacefully in her sleep shortly after that trip, her demise totally unrelated to eating the sandwich. Back alone in my apartment and nervously popping chocolates after my pleasant, unexpected outing with Cliff Jentzen, I had a vivid flashback of that day with Ellewina. She would have liked him, I thought, even though he had ended an otherwise swell afternoon on a crummy note of vagueness by mumbling the three most dreaded words in the male vocabulary: "I'll call you."

I casually flipped on the TV, catching the tail end of *Entertainment Tonight*. I was just in time to hear perky Mary Hart pose a disconcerting question—"Where's Marcy?" As the screen showed the well-worn tape of me angrily throwing the ring at Neil the other night, she provided viewers with this gripping status report:

"Offers of television deals and commercial endorsements keep pouring in for Marcy Lee Mallowitz, the thirty-four-year-old Personal Life Coach whose feisty response to getting ditched by her orthodontist boyfriend on *So You Want to Be Filthy Rich!* the other night won the nation's hearts and admiration. But in a puzzling first that is said to have even close friends scratching their heads, this television natural seems reluctant to step into the spotlight, choosing, at least for now, to remain holed up incommunicado in her Greenwich Village apartment. Mental health experts consulted by *ET* were divided on whether her aberrant behavior indicates a pathologically weak or strong sense of self. Among the many offers and invitations awaiting her response is one to appear at a star-studded cocktail fundraising reception in Los Angeles next month for BIG TV's NOW, a charitable group working to bridge the nation's entertainment divide by selling name-brand projection television sets on a discount basis to poor families whose present TV is more than two years old and has a screen size under thirty-six inches. Tomorrow, in an *ET* exclusive, we will examine this new phenomenon of reality-show fame, and delve into the history and implications of the ongoing story some leading media critics are now calling 'Marcygate.' "

Marcygate? I said to myself as I reached for the remote and pressed the off button in disgust.

Watergate and Monicagate I get. But what did I ever do to deserve Marcygate? I've never taken part in a burglary or abused people's civil liberties. Nor have I ever had sex with a president inside the Oval Office. Ditto outside the Oval Office. Of course, I don't claim to speak for my good friend Lois.

All but one of these talented comics was featured on the ill-fated Mary Tyler Moore variety show, *Mary*, that was canceled after only three airings. Who avoided the fiasco?

a. David Letterman
b. David Brenner
c. Dick Shawn
d. Michael Keaton

See correct answer on back. . . .

ANSWER

◆

b. David Brenner

Ten

✦

When I got up the next day, it was already well past noon. My delay in rising let me enjoy a vivid dream that I was back on *Filthy Rich!* with Neil, the creep, and everything was unfolding just as it really had. I still messed up on Teri Garr, only instead of harmlessly throwing the piddling ring, I threw Kingman's bulky game monitor, which Kingman ripped off its base and kindly handed to me, saying, "I don't like that guy." In my dream, I effortlessly hurled the monitor at Neil's rotten head, instantly causing him to drop to the ground, dying, as the audience stood in unison wildly applauding my bold gesture.

The downer was awakening to find that it was only a dream, and that my overflowing message tape contained no messages from my eBay savior, Cliff Jentzen—the one potential bright spot on my otherwise bleak social horizon. It left me feeling as dark as the deep gray areas that now dotted the once pink Rosie sweats I was still wearing, and I responded in the same mature way I usually do when I'm feeling that depressed. I ate everything fattening in sight, and that was a lot, given the week's still-mounting haul of gourmet freebies. Then, I crawled back into bed and fell into a comalike sleep, which, disappointingly for me, produced no new dreams of Neil's violent death.

It was three days since Neil had dumped me, and I was going to the dogs.

I suspect, though obviously I have no way of proving it, that it was Ellewina's ghostly spirit rather than an urgent need to relieve myself that caused me to reawaken suddenly at around eleven-thirty that night, and grab for the remote to tune in to *Late Show with David Letterman*. Normally, I do my best to avoid David Letterman. His much publicized bypass operation was supposed to make him nicer, but it hasn't happened. Plus, not to seem mean myself, I don't get what he's up to with his hair—what there is of it, I mean. My mother, for what it's worth, thinks his bandleader, "that sweetie" Paul Schaffer, should have left the show long ago.

Anyway, there was yucky, disgusting, double-crossing Neil on *Letterman*.

He appeared near the beginning of the show, dressed in his crisp, ultra-white dental jacket, which amused Dave and led to one of his snide asides: "Hey, help me out here. Is this guy really an orthodontist? I'm asking, because to me, anyway, he looks like the Good Humor man. Am I right on that, Paul?"

"Definitely," replied the bandleader. "Pretty groovy."

Maybe Letterman isn't so bad after all, I decided. He was right. Neil did look like the Good Humor man.

But Letterman's ribbing didn't seem to be spoiling Neil's good time. My oblivious ex was still smiling broadly as he stood in the spotlight, his apparent joy in being included on the hip nighttime show totally undiminished. He was there to read the evening's Top Ten List.

· ·

TOP TEN REASONS TO CHOOSE MARCY LEE MALLOWITZ AS YOUR LIFELINE

· ·

10. You're a masochist and just love losing $1.75 million.

9. She's great in bed.

8. She has the same initials as Marilyn Monroe, the Greatest Lifeline of All.

7. You got the show's name wrong. You thought it was *So You Want to Go Down the Toilet!*

6. Kingman promised no questions about Sonny and Cher.

5. Your real Personal Life Coach was busy that night.

4. You had no choice. You were told it was either her or the insane Australian guy on cable who plays with crocodiles.

3. It may be a cheap ring, but you want it back really, really badly.

2. When Kingman said choose a Lifeline, you thought she'd just be reading palms.

And the Number One Reason to Choose Marcy Lee Mallowitz as Your Lifeline?

    1. Her mother's fat-filled cooking, stupid.

"Nicely done," said Dave.

Nicely done, indeed.

I was not amused. Neither, let me assure you, was my mother, who was watching—but with none of the customary kvelling—back in Brooklyn.

My first reaction was horror and disbelief. I must have sat there in bed, completely frozen, for a full five minutes.

My second reaction was to dip into the giant tin of dark chocolate butter-crunch squares, which Mike Wallace and his *60 Minutes* producers had collectively sent over earlier in the day, no doubt hoping to gain an edge over the upstarts at *60 Minutes II,* whose skimpy offering of a few Pepperidge Farm cookie assortments served merely to reinforce my long-standing worries about the future of TV news. In less than a minute of devouring the Mike Wallace butter crunch, my back teeth were pretty much stuck together, and a brown, nutty drool began cascading from the right corner of my mouth. It ran down my chin, until a big glob fell on my once-pink sweatshirt from Rosie O'Donnell, all but obscuring the distinctive Rosie logo. For the first time since losing Neil on *Filthy Rich!* I began to cry, and couldn't seem to stop. It was my lowest moment.

Then something remarkable happened. Something I

thought only happens in low-budget movies when the screenwriter has had a bad day and is rushing to get home. A faint voice inside my head—old Ellewina's, I presumed— told me this was no time to be crying and drooling. Why let that tooth-moving piece of decay, Neil, have the last word, and ruin your reputation? Don't sit around feeling sorry for yourself, kid. Wake up and sniff the sauces.

Sniff the sauces. On the word "sauces" I had a revelation. Amid all the deliveries I received the Day After, I suddenly recalled a small but tasty box of imported pistachio nuts. It came with a small card, which read as follows: "Hope you'll do the show. Dave." No doubt Neil had received the same package. My ego was so bloated by my own avid courting by the media, it hadn't occurred to me that Neil, the crumb, was simultaneously getting many of the same invitations and offers, and, worse, might actually accept some of them. At that very moment, for all I knew, Neil was lounging around in a Rosie O'Donnell sweatsuit identical to the one I still had on—except his was probably in navy blue and smelled a whole lot better than mine did at that particular point.

Not Oprah, I thought. Please say Oprah's personal chef didn't cook for Neil. But Neil, the scum, had already abused my good name on *Letterman*. Who could say where on the dial he'd show up next?

This was War, and I needed a game plan. So I did what any red-blooded American female would do under the circumstances. I dialed my two best girlfriends, Norma and Lois, and arranged a secret 1 A.M. strategy meeting at a favorite East Village restaurant, the Life Cafe, at the corner of Tenth Street and Avenue B. It wasn't the most convenient choice. But Lois, who was still clad in a long Donna Karan sheath, had just returned from a stirring Democratic Party salute to Buddhist fund-raisers, where they served only meager appetizers consistent with a vow of poverty. She was feeling a craving for the cafe's vegan nachos.

I could feel my old determination begin to return as I peeled off the Rosie sweatsuit that had been my security blanket for three days, and hopped into the shower. The world looks a lot better when you have clean hair, I thought as I quickly toweled off. It's one of the first rules I teach my Personal Life Coaching clients—Rule Number Three, to be exact, on the convenient wallet-size handout I call "Marcy's Magnificent Seven." Number One, in case you're wondering, is "Remember to floss," and was, quite obviously, rotten Neil's contribution to the enterprise. You can quibble with its placement in the order, but after mulling it over while I finished blow-drying my hair, I decided flossing is still important for both appearance and fresh breath, and downgrading it on my list would just confuse any clients I still had remaining when I finally got back to work, and it would look vindictive besides.

Figuring this was a conspiratorial gathering I was heading to, and wanting to blend in with the night, I opted for an all-black look—elegant, if suddenly hard-to-zip black Calvin Klein slacks, black scooped-neck tee with three-quarter-length sleeves, and a black cardigan with dark mother-of-pearl buttons that I bought years ago when all the fashion magazines were predicting that the country-club look was coming back. Black everything. Even black underwear. Everything black, that is, except for the purple bandanna and sunglasses that Cliff had left behind, and I decided those still made sense as an antipaparazzi precaution.

"That you, Ms. Mallowitz?" said the night doorman, Al, when I appeared in the lobby. "Feeling better?"

"I think so, Al," I said. "I'll know more after my stroll."

I hadn't been out this late without a man in three years, and going out the door by myself this first time felt scary, but also strangely liberating. My goal was to briskly walk the seven crosstown blocks from my apartment to the Life Cafe, thereby achieving a mild aerobic workout. Despite the recent drop in crime, I know it's not prudent for a woman to be walking alone past midnight when the streets can get pretty deserted, even in all-night Greenwich Village. But three days spent mostly cooped up and eating like a sumo wrestler trying to achieve a higher weight class had left me feeling flabby and exercise deprived. I was anxious to make up for lost time.

As I exited my building on Fifth Avenue, I noticed a navy blue Lincoln Town Car parked right out front. It was just sitting there, its lights out and its dark-tinted windows rolled up tight, as if the big, red "No Standing" sign rising from the sidewalk did not apply. I didn't think much of it—there are even more Town Cars in the city than Gap stores, and if God meant man to obey parking rules, as far as I'm concerned, he would have commanded parking-garage owners not to charge as much as $29.50 an hour in some parts of Manhattan. Besides, at that moment I was preoccupied, mentally kicking myself for forgetting the small hand weights I'd meant to carry to turn this little nighttime hike into a legitimate Powerwalk. On the bright side, I told myself, the fact you're so upset means you're back to thinking like a Personal Life Coach. In the process, I was again observing Rule Number Three on Marcy's Magnificent Seven, which is easy to remember because it also happens to be the title of a well-known song: "Keep Your Sunny Side Up." As I always tell my clients: The best way to nurture your sunny side (apart from clean, shiny hair) is regular exercise, preferably a combination of aerobic and strength training at least three or four times a week. Try it! It's also great for the skin and staying trim!

Anyway, back to the parked Town Car in front of my building. As I was saying, it barely made an impression. But as I turned the corner to head east on Tenth Street, I developed the distinct feeling I was being followed. I started stepping faster, feeling fortunate I had chosen to wear my black Reeboks instead of the Ferragamo loafers I had forcibly wrested from another customer's hands at a recent sale, causing something of a scene.

Immediately, I began feeling like an idiot, although not

for grabbing the shoes. (Lest you think badly of me, I should tell you that my competitor had been standing in such a way as to block everyone else's access to the sale table for at least five minutes, making my aggressive seizure fully justified.) However, I did feel like an idiot for running. Stay calm. It's just your imagination playing tricks, I told myself. It's misty out, and wearing dark sunglasses at night can be disorienting. But events quickly confirmed that more was at work here than Cliff's old Ray-Bans.

The Town Car, suddenly alive, had just headed around the corner and was moving slowly along the curb in my direction.

My walk now became a run. I still held out a hope that it was just my imagination, that the blue Lincoln would make a turn when we reached the corner of Tenth and University Place. Instead, the mystery car kept pace a few feet behind, following my bad example as I crossed the street illegally against a red light. On an impulse, I now turned around and started running in the opposite direction, back toward my apartment. But the Town Car would not be so easily eluded. Whoever was driving just put it in reverse, then slammed on the gas to catch up to me, heading the wrong way down the nearly empty one-way street. When the car was about even with me, the back window rolled down halfway, and I heard a man calling my name in a loud stage whisper.

"Marcy. Marcy get over here. It's me."

I stopped to look but didn't say anything. I still couldn't see who was talking.

"Marcy, over here. It's me, Kingman. Kingman Fenimore. I need to talk to you."

He rolled the window down farther, so I could confirm the ID.

Much to my amazement, it really was Kingman Fenimore. I could see that now. But what was he doing here on East Tenth Street, scaring the wits out of Marcy Lee Mallowitz at this ungodly hour on a weekday night? I wondered. Why wasn't he at home in bed getting rested to appear live at 9 A.M. as host of the phenomenally successful daytime gig that preceded his prime-time *Filthy Rich!* success? By that, of course, I'm referring to *Gabbing! With Kingman and Tracy Ellen*. Honestly, I'd never seen it, in keeping with Rule Number Five of Marcy's Magnificent Seven: "Watching daytime TV is degenerate." But I knew the imminent departure of Tracy Ellen, who was leaving to bring her special blend of folksy family stories and racy double-entendre humor to a new show the Christian Broadcasting Network was planning for her, had triggered a major nationwide talent search to find a replacement.

Personally, I was pretty sick of hearing about it. It seemed you couldn't pick up a newspaper without reading something about Kingman and *Filthy Rich!* or the daily ups and downs in the ongoing hunt for a new Tracy Ellen. Goodness, even the new surgically improved Linda Tripp was being considered for a tryout. Who next, Paula Jones? Fawn Hall? Kato Kaelin? After almost forty years in show business, including three demeaning years in the mid-eighties that saw him eke out a living turning letters on *Wheel of Fortune* when Vanna White was vacationing, Kingman Fenimore's time had finally arrived.

In fact, that's exactly what Kingman told me when I accepted his invitation of a lift, and slid into the seat beside him in the Town Car's roomy backseat.

"This is my time!" said Kingman, displaying the same genial bombast he uses to great effect on TV. "They're paying me twenty-two million a year, and I'm single-handedly keeping alive an entire network. With a stupid game show, can you believe it? At my age?"

He then turned serious. "But something's come up, Marcy. Believe me, I don't usually skulk around Greenwich Village following attractive young women like yourself. I'm happily married. But I need your help."

He handed me an official-looking twenty-odd-page report.

"The new ratings numbers," he said. "They won't be public until tomorrow morning, but they're giving me a bad headache already. Driver, you have a couple of spare Advils up there?"

"Sorry, Mr. Fenimore," said the driver. "You finished my last headache stuff about an hour ago."

"I'd settle for a stiff drink, but I don't want people to start talking if I happen to slur words one night on *Filthy Rich!*," said Kingman, segueing into an imitation of an inebriated host delivering the familiar line, "Is that your absolute answer?" "I'm swimming with sharks, Marcy. Sharks, I tell you."

"But everyone loves you, Kingman," I said. "Even Letterman is nice to you."

"Letterman. If he's such a good friend, why did he send a taped segment for my last birthday instead of waking up early to wish me well on the morning show with Tracy Ellen? And this cockamamie search for Tracy Ellen's replacement. Let's not even go *there*."

By then, we'd been kibitzing about half an hour, circling the restaurant six or seven times. Seeing the Life Cafe go by again, I shared my concern that Lois and Norma were waiting for me, and were apt to call the police if I didn't arrive soon, which could be pretty embarrassing all around, especially after my minor dustup at Ferragamo.

"Look at this," Kingman said, pointing to a bunch of figures buried in the middle of the report. "They're going to have a field day with this."

What the numbers showed, Kingman explained, was that *The Plank,* the pseudo pirates/executives survival show up against *Filthy Rich!* two days a week on a competing network, was now attracting millions more viewers. In other words, *Filthy Rich!,* that seemingly indomitable nighttime colossus, had slipped from number one in the ratings. The demographics were even more dire, with *The Plank* killing *Filthy Rich!* in the critical competition for the eighteen- to thirty-five-year-old viewers that advertisers most covet. Even the other truly awful "reality" show that follows *The Plank*—the one featuring the exciting doings on a luxury cruise ship pop-

ulated by two dozen well-tanned seniors from Miami—
scored better than Kingman's show among younger viewers. If you haven't seen it, think an elderly *Love Boat*
without those finely crafted scripts, and featuring a thick-
ened Gopher behind the bar serving up tall glasses of
Ensure with those cute little paper umbrellas.

Why this sudden fall from grace?

Kingman didn't get it. He was frustrated, and it caused
him to launch into a little rant.

"What's so great about *The Plank*? They say it's more
'real' than *Filthy Rich!* Have you seen it? We're talking network people dressed in costumes left over from an old
DeMille epic yelling, 'Shiver me timbers.' It's filmed in
Burbank, for Chrissakes. Burbank! Ever been to Burbank?
It makes Los Angeles look like bucolic, open countryside.
And those rats they eat? They're from Spago, I swear. Check
out the credits. Can you believe it, the show simulates hard-
ship on a remote tropical island by hiring Wolfgang Puck as
the official food consultant. That's not what I call *real* entertainment. It's not even *real* cuisine."

The polling data Kingman showed me didn't mention
Spago or Wolfgang Puck. It suggested instead that *Filthy
Rich!* was lagging badly owing mainly to a shortage of contestants with a high likability quotient, or Q rating, and
insufficient real-life drama. I understood why Kingman was
agitated. For a comparatively high-quality effort like *Filthy
Rich!* to lose out to boring drivel like *The Plank* wasn't just
insulting, it was damned unfair.

"They want drama. I'm going to give them drama," Kingman said. "Marcy, that's where you come in."

While Neil's Q rating fell somewhere in the zero range, it turned out that my rating was astronomical. "The audience loved you, Marcy, the way you think Letterman loves me," Kingman said. "Only in your case, it's actually true."

Kingman's plan, which he wanted my permission to announce at a news conference already scheduled for the late morning, called for me to make a much-heralded return to *Filthy Rich!* in just twenty-one days—as a contestant this time, not a piddling Lifeline. The "bounce" from my appearance and all the preshow publicity it was bound to generate, he figured, would be enough to reclaim the number one spot for at least a few weeks, at which point he'd just have to come up with another desperate plan in the event public enthusiasm for *The Plank* didn't cool down.

The scheme had some obvious pluses. It would be my chance to help out Kingman, avenge Neil's mistreatment of me, and, potentially, take home buckets of ready cash. But Kingman made it clear I'd have to agree to a big publicity buildup in advance—the cover of *TV Guide, Newsweek, Entertainment Weekly,* and appearances on all the major talk shows. The works! "No more hiding, Marcy. And that babushka thing you have on your head," he said in reference to the purple bandanna from Cliff, "it has to go."

"I'll do it," I found myself saying as the car came to a stop in front of the restaurant. "I'll do it."

I know this is not the sort of life-transforming decision

you should make on impulse, or, in my case, without channeling Marcia Brady. But I really liked Kingman, and I wanted to help him prolong his stay at the top. Of course, I also wanted the money. And although personally clueless as to the likely ratings implications, I admit I also liked his plan to showcase me. Kingman's idea for my triumphant return to *Filthy Rich!* struck me as a dignified act of redemption, in a wholly different league tastewise from Whoopi's proffered Hollywood square. I was sure it would strike the public that way, too.

"But there's one condition," I added.

"Anything, Marcy," Kingman said. "I liked you from the start. Your mother, too. The orthodontist, I don't like that guy." Funny, Kingman said exactly the same thing in my dream.

"The deal, Kingman, is I get to choose my own Lifeline," I said, sounding alarmingly like Tom Cruise in the movie about the sports agent, *Jerry Maguire*, and providing a live example of Rule Number Six on Marcy's Magnificent Seven: "Big elbows are always in fashion."

"I mean it, Kingman. My Lifeline. Just like it was a regular show. You don't choose for me."

"Deal," said Kingman as I started getting out of the car. "And, oh, one thing, Marcy. You may want to eat fast. Diane Sawyer will be at your apartment with a *Good Morning America* crew at about six A.M. to set up for a live interview. I took the liberty of arranging it to get things rolling this morning."

How could Kingman be so presumptuous? I started to tell him he'd have to cancel Diane Sawyer. I couldn't possibly get me and my place ready to welcome her and her cameras on so little notice. But I soon realized I was standing on the sidewalk talking to myself, Kingman and his navy blue Town Car having already disappeared into the night.

Eva Gabor, whose underrated comedic skills lit up *Green Acres*, had two sisters, the most famous of which, of course, was Zsa Zsa. What was her other sister's name?

a. Jolie
b. Tina
c. Alessandra
d. Magda

See correct answer on back. . . .

ANSWER

✦

d. Magda

Eleven

◆

"Oh shit. What have I done?"

I was so amazed and appalled by the commitment I had just made to Kingman Fenimore that I said the words out loud. Emphasis on "loud." It was entirely involuntary.

"Oh shit."

"Marcy, we're back here," yelled Norma equally loudly across the darkly lit and largely deserted restaurant. "What took you so long? You look like a walking train wreck."

That's why I love Norma, I thought. She's always bucking me up.

Reaching the corner table she and Lois had staked out, I detected tiny corn chip crumbs on the large, otherwise barren plate sitting in front of Lois, suggesting that while I was being wooed by Kingman Fenimore for a ratings-smashing return to *Filthy Rich!,* she was devouring a large order of nachos with extra soy cheese. Another empty plate near Norma held the crusty remains of my feminist pal's usual veggie burger and fries. A third plate near my seat held a half-eaten serving of the cafe's tasty brown rice and tofu dish. Apparently, Norma and Lois had ordered it for me in the hope of getting me back on a healthy regimen following my three-day pig-out, only to pig out a wee bit themselves, jointly picking at my meal when I didn't appear. Not that I could blame them. Their picking aside, I appreciated my friends' gentle effort to remind me about Rule Number Two on Marcy's Magnificent Seven: "Shun fattening foods."

"You're very late," said Lois, still in her evening gown and three-inch Prada heels that make her walk like Bette Midler. "We couldn't wait. I was starving."

I was dying to tell my news, but I didn't want to interrupt Lois, who was prattling on about a bright idea she had for improving the Democrats' catering in the post-Clinton-Gore era. "Why is it that when my Jewish donors throw a party, there's way too much food, yet at a Buddhist do like the one tonight, you're lucky if you see a stale little pretzel stick with a tiny bowl of dip? Would it be politically incorrect if I sent a memo to the Democratic National Committee in Washington suggesting we combine our Jewish and Buddhist fund-raising divisions? People could mix, and we'd get the food just right."

"Great idea, Lois," said Norma rather dismissively. "You and your letters." Norma proceeded to recall one Lois had written her sophomore year in college, chastising the Nobel committee for overlooking Maybelline's introduction of new, waterproof, longer-lash mascara. "Let Marcy talk," she said.

Personally, I thought Lois might be on to something this time. If the Dems are ever to regain the White House, big donors can't be sent home hungry. Nonetheless, I was pleased to get the floor. I described my unexpected Town Car encounter with Kingman, and announced to my friends that I had agreed to return to *Filthy Rich!* in three weeks as a contestant. They both seemed pretty excited, although for different reasons. Norma saw it as my chance to show up Neil and advance the feminist cause. Lois thought it an opportunity to show up Neil and meet great guys.

"How about your Lifeline?" Norma asked. "If you want, I'll be your Lifeline, even though you know I hate the show for having so few women contestants. It just reinforces stereotypes about women not being as smart or competitive as men, and helps perpetuate the discriminatory economic pecking order by creating all those new male millionaires."

"Calm down, Norma. This is *us* you're addressing, not some *Nightline* panel on the vital issue of sexism and TV game shows," said Lois, adding, "If you ask me, I think the world could use a few *more* male millionaires."

"And, Lois, that's why the Democrats are lucky to have you," said Norma.

"Go back to your corners, ladies," I said.

"I didn't start it," said Norma. "I'm just thinking aloud that going on the show would make me look like a giant hypocrite, having just bashed the anti-feminist message of the so-called reality shows in *The New York Review of Books*. Come to think of it, Marcy, I can't be your Lifeline, can I?"

"I'd be your Lifeline, if you want," said Lois.

"Thanks," I said. "The two of you would be great. But I wouldn't take either of you as my Lifeline. Look what happened when I blew it for Neil."

"*You* didn't blow it. *Neil's* the one who blew it," said Lois.

"Thanks, but obviously Neil didn't think so," I said. "All I'm saying is that you're my two best friends in the world and I don't want to risk our friendship by relying on you as my Lifeline. Not to be sappy, but once burned, twice an idiot."

"*Neil's* the only idiot here," said Lois.

"Right," said Norma. "Marcy, I warned you about him from the start."

I looked at my watch. It was just after 2 A.M.

"I'd love to continue this pleasant chitchat, ladies, but I have to go," I said, rising from my chair.

"You practically just arrived," said Norma. "Sit," she ordered. "I have big news, too."

Her news was that her publisher was so impressed by sales of her new feminist opus, the firm had decided to issue a new, updated audiotape edition of her controversial second best-seller, a feminist treatise on modern marriage called *Fourth-Finger Itch*. "They've hired Dame Judi Dench to be the reader. I can't wait to meet her," said Norma.

"Exciting," I said. Of course, what I was really thinking was that the very dignified Dame Judi obviously hadn't read the book, or she would never have agreed to recite its racy section on unbiased ways to keep the fun in marital sex. I was also thinking that Diane Sawyer and her crew would be arriving at my apartment in exactly four hours and the place was a wreck. I was even more of a wreck. My right hand reached up to my scalp and began tugging hard on a clump of hair, much as it always does just as panic begins to set in.

I quickly explained my predicament, and stood to leave.

"Wait, kid, we're coming," said Lois, tugging at Norma's sleeve to get her up. "We're a team. Like in *The Three Musketeers*."

"Lois, get it straight," said Norma, resurrecting an old tiff. "They didn't allow female musketeers. Why is it your literary references include no women authors?"

"Because there were only *two* Brontë sisters, okay?" said Lois. "And because the alternate choice was *The Three Little Pigs*. Besides, I meant *Three Musketeers* only in a metaphorical sense. Right, Marcy?"

I decided it was best not to take sides.

"Look, I could use your help," I said. "But don't feel obligated, guys."

"Are you kidding, Marcy? I wouldn't miss it," said Norma, reaching over to grab the check from the middle of the table and hand it to Lois. "I believe it's your turn, my chivalrous musketeer. I'll do the tip."

As we exited the restaurant together, a *Daily News* truck pulled alongside the newsstand on the corner and dropped two big bundles of the morning paper on the sidewalk. I walked over to check out the front page, and when I saw it, I almost plotzed.

There in glorious black and white was the picture of me posing with the owner of that Chinese restaurant in Astoria, the one Cliff Jentzen had taken me to. And to think I assumed the photo would just hang by the front entrance, with Tony Bennett. Boy, was I ever naive. Norma, who is normally pretty canny when it comes to such matters, observed that the money the *News* paid for the shot would buy a lot of Moo Goo Gai Pan.

In the picture, I was smiling. At least that was some consolation.

Underneath it was a big caption, "Marcy's Day Out," followed by this little tidbit of non-news: "Just three days after getting dumped by her orthodontist boyfriend on the top-rated *So You Want to Be Filthy Rich!* Marcy Lee Mallowitz finally left her apartment yesterday to make a secret lunch stop at a Chinese restaurant in Queens. The owner (shown here) says she was accompanied by an unidentified male friend, and the two of them huddled close and shared dishes. How long can Marcy hide the identity of this mystery man?"

Probably forever, I thought, since he'll never call me now. He said he hates this celebrity stuff, and with my imminent return to *Filthy Rich!* about to be announced, it was going to get a lot worse.

"So who's the guy?" Lois said. "Someone we know? Were you two-timing Neil? Good for you, girl. Go, Marcy."

"No, I never cheated on Neil when we were together. It's nothing that interesting. The guy is just someone I met. No big deal. If our lunch didn't scare him off, I'm sure this will."

We decided to hail a taxi, husbanding our strength to prepare for my imminent rendezvous with Diane Sawyer.

Once ensconced in the cab's backseat, Lois and I fell into our old, loopy game of trying to decide the *Brady Bunch* episode most applicable to the current situation. Lois nominated the episode where Marcia wants to be in the school variety show, and her mom, dad, and brother Greg somehow wind up in it, too. Episode Eighty-one.

"I was thinking the same thing," I said. "Just substitute me for Marcia, and *Good Morning America* for the school show, and you have a pretty similar plot. And I guess you two symbolize the other Bradys, only instead of actually being in the show, you're just helping me straighten. Makes sense."

"Can someone open a window, please?" said Norma, squeezed uncomfortably between the two of us. "This conversation is making me carsick."

What was the name of the Brooklyn high school where the John Travolta character Vinnie Barbarino and the other underachieving "sweathogs" enlivened classes on *Welcome Back, Kotter*?

a. Millard Fillmore High
b. George Washington High
c. James Buchanan High
d. Grover Cleveland High

See correct answer on back. . . .

```
..............................................................

         A N S W E R

              ◆

    c. James Buchanan High

..............................................................
```

Twelve

✦

"*It's a disaster* area," I cautioned my two intrepid sidekicks as we entered my apartment. "Don't make fun. It's been a bad week."

"I've seen worse," said Norma, coolly eyeing the empty Godiva boxes, fancy cookie tins, wilted floral offerings, rotting fruit baskets, crumbled chips bags, plates of half-eaten pizza slices, and cellophane sandwich wrappers bespeaking multiple deli deliveries that now constituted my home decor. Oh, and I forgot the ample scattering of white pistachio shells and plastic twenty-ounce bottles of Coke. When I'm depressed, only The Real Thing will do. For medicinal powers, I find, Diet Coke just can't compete, though for three years I refrained from acting on that observation out of respect for Neil's crusade against sugary sodas and their nefarious role in promoting tooth decay.

"Norma's right," said Lois. "We've seen worse. Remember the mess after the all-night year-end party we threw in our dorm suite with those Columbia guys freshman year?"

"How could I forget?" I said. Barnard's dean put us on academic probation until we ponied up for the large window accidentally broken when some brainy male guests got the bright idea of playing catch blindfolded using an empty beer keg. The guys who co-sponsored this elegant soiree received no reprimand from the Columbia dean, a galling injustice that I believe was influential in shaping Norma's feminist ideology.

"This is nothing compared to that," said Lois. "You haven't broken any windows."

"Great," I said, stepping carefully around the empty pints of Ben & Jerry's Double Chocolate Chocolate Chip that dotted the floor of my living room and bedroom like so many gooey grenades. Why is it that some intelligent, highly educated career women react to personal traumas by turning their normally neat living quarters into veritable pigpens? Maybe Norma can examine the phenomenon in her next book, I started thinking, only to be interrupted by the feminist author herself.

"Marcy, snap out of it," she roared. "Get a grip. You're a Personal Life Coach. Tell us what to do."

I was grateful for the reprimand. "You're right," I said. "Let's get busy."

I assigned Lois to work with me picking up the pieces of debris defiling my apartment, and tossing them in a large green trash bag. Except, that is, for the Coke bottles, which we tossed into a special blue plastic bag for recyclables, mindful that the environment shouldn't suffer just because of my fragile emotional state. Lois performed this pickup without complaint, notwithstanding the sheer volume, and the obvious difficulty she had bending in her tight designer gown. Moreover, it was a wonder she avoided slipping and breaking a limb traipsing around the littered floors in her stockinged feet. That's loyalty, I thought, working beside her. I was very touched.

But if there were a Gold Medal for loyalty, it would have to go to Norma. She followed Lois and me around with the vacuum, amiably performing a form of tedious low-level housework—generally considered "women's work"—that surely would have offended her feminist sensibilities, potentially inspiring a picket line, were it not for our bond of friendship.

When that was done, Norma made the command decision to rejuvenate our flagging energy by loading my *Grease* sound track into the stereo, and turning up the volume until the whole place seemed to vibrate. The three of us picked up dust rags and began to bop around the apartment to the sound of the young Travolta, mouthing the words and pausing regularly to aggressively polish all adjacent surfaces. By about 4 A.M., the place was looking a lot better and reeking of lemon Pledge.

It was about this time that Lois unilaterally decided that pausing during my interview to offer Diane Sawyer home-baked cookies would add a homey touch that could only enhance my standing with viewers. After a quick trip to an all-night Korean market for ingredients, Lois took over my small kitchen, sending the smell of baking Toll House cookies wafting through the apartment and weakening my newly renewed resolve to observe the oft-violated Rule Number Two of Marcy's Magnificent Seven: "Shun fattening foods."

While Lois was contentedly playing Betty Crocker in the kitchen, Norma, by now an old TV hand, started briefing me on the questions Diane Sawyer was likely to ask, and telling me how I should answer. The briefing continued once I got out of the shower, and Lois, in between batches of cookies, was blow-drying my hair, which made it kind of hard to hear.

Wielding a round styling brush, Lois was trying to undo the great Giovanni's damage by tucking under the ends of my multilayered shoulder-length mop, an uphill quest she hoped would eventually reveal my missing cheekbones, and achieve the youthful yet sophisticated fashion look my celebrated stylist had promised in that lilting Italian accent of his, and then woefully failed to deliver. But my hair wouldn't cooperate. The right side went under all right, but on the left, each defiant layer kept separately popping up, creating multiple flips that left me looking like a stranded extra from an old Elvis movie.

Fortunately, we had better luck with my clothes. Rummaging through my closet and drawers, we found a perfect informal outfit for a morning show: a straight khaki skirt with a simple periwinkle-blue collared shirt that would show up well on television—both Banana Republic. There was a nervous moment when I tried to put the skirt on and found, after three days of bingeing, that I couldn't button it, but Norma eventually saved the day, successfully pulling up the front zipper and closing the snap while Lois pressed my stomach in and I held my breath. We spontaneously broke out in giggles and exchanged enthusiastic high fives. Miraculously, my skirt stayed buttoned during this activity, but I maturely decided not to tempt Fate by eating one of Lois's cookies before the show.

Next my makeup. Diane Sawyer wasn't scheduled to arrive for another hour and a half. But Lois and Norma thought it best to get an early start, given the daunting beauty challenge posed by the flaking, dry skin and criss-crossing fine lines wrought by my emotional turmoil, plus the pitch-black rings under my eyes that brought to mind the dalmatians who tormented Glenn Close.

Beginning this beautification project, I was reminded of Rule Number Four on Marcy's Magnificent Seven: "Moisturize." By including "Moisturize" on my short list, by the way, my intention was to emphasize the importance of moist skin for a vibrant, healthy appearance and to slow the aging process. I did not mean to minimize the crucial need to exfoliate your skin prior to applying your moisturizer—preferably a light, creamy formula made with only natural ingredients, though you needn't spend a fortune on high-priced brands like La Mer. One interesting historical note.

Originally Rule Number Four had two parts, "Moisturize" *and* "Avoid wearing horizontal stripes." But Norma found this offensive. She complained bitterly that offering what amounted to eight rules as my Magnificent Seven would further societal stereotypes about women being bad at math. So I foreswore commenting about the stripes, with the disconcerting result that I have several clients who still run around town looking like humongous mobile flags.

Around 5 A.M., just as my makeup job was nearing completion and I was almost looking human, there was an unexpected knock. It was my morning doorman, Frank, who was just beginning his shift. He said some neighbors had called downstairs to complain about noise coming from my apartment, so he'd come up to check.

"Everything okay, Miss Mallowitz?" he said, looking around.

"Fine, Frank. You can assure the neighbors there'll be no more late-night vacuuming or dance parties." I explained that the noisy cleanup owed only to Diane Sawyer's imminent arrival.

"Diane Sawyer?" Frank said. "When?"

I checked my watch. "We're at T minus fifty-five minutes and counting."

"Almost a full hour, then. Good," said Frank, barging right past me and into the apartment. "That still gives us time to do something about the furniture."

"The furniture?" said Lois, emerging from her cookie duty in the kitchen, a red-checkered apron tied over her designer gown. "What's wrong with the furniture? Some of it she got from me when I upgraded after my divorce."

"It's out of harmony," said my doorman.

It turned out Frank was taking a New School class in feng shui—the ancient Chinese science of arranging furniture and color schemes in alignment with nature—and I was to be the first beneficiary. I knew little about feng shui other than that it was all the rage among interior decorators serving the spiritual Upper East Side and the quaint if crowded Long Island towns comprising what I think of as the Greater Hamptons Region. But I was open-minded.

The same cannot be said of Lois. Still peeved about the implied slur on her former furniture, she only half-kiddingly bombarded Frank with cynical questions about his credentials. "How do we know you're a qualified feng shui person?" she teased Frank. "Is it like karate? Do you get a black belt or anything?"

"Ignore Lois," I told Frank. "I don't want to be out of harmony when I meet Diane Sawyer."

"No bother, I'm used to skeptics," said Frank. "My own mother glued down her furniture to keep me from touching anything."

As this exchange was transpiring, Frank was purposefully moving about the living room, fluffing pillows and changing the angle of the sofa in relation to the windows and the comfy, if bulky-looking dark green velvet sitting chair from Lois that I liked to curl up in for reading. It was just a small change. But even Lois had to admit it was an improvement, having the effect of making the room seem bigger and more open.

"Cookie?" she said to Frank, tendering a sample from her Toll House project in a gesture of friendship.

"Delicious," said Frank, taking a bite. "It would make sense feng shui–wise to have them out when Diane Sawyer is doing the interview."

"Exactly what I told Marcy," said Lois. "Maybe there *is* something to this feng shui stuff." She pronounced it feng sooey.

"That's *shway,* Lois, with an *h,*" corrected Norma. "One syllable. Rhymes with 'hay.' " Then to Frank: "What else? There's not much time left."

"You sure you want to hear?" said Frank.

"Frank, we're grown-ups. We can take it," said Norma.

"Okay, then," Frank said. "But you're not going to like it."

His bottom line was that my living room chair was too dark and heavy. It had to go. "We've got to find another," he said.

"Furniture shopping at this hour?" I said. "The corner deli has a good salad bar, but I don't think it delivers living room chairs yet."

"No problem. I know just the thing," Frank said. "It's in Mrs. Schwartz's apartment. We can go get it."

I was confused. "Since when has my cranky neighbor gone into the all-night furniture business?" I said.

Mrs. Schwartz was away, Frank explained. She'd flown down to Boca Raton with her sister to join Richard Simmons for a special weight-and-fitness program for people over sixty-five, called "Rolling *with* the Oldies" by the weird fitness guru to distinguish it from the more active "Rolling *to* the Oldies" you've seen advertised in late-night infomercials. The mention of Richard Simmons caused Lois to chime in with a savvy if irrelevant observation I was pretty sure she didn't pick up on *The Brady Bunch*.

"Hairy men shouldn't wear tank tops," she said.

"Why just tell *us*?" said Norma. "You should write one of your letters, Lois. I'm sure Richard Simmons would be very interested. Not to mention the whole tank-top industry."

But back to the story. Before going away, Mrs. Schwartz had put Frank in charge of feeding, walking, and otherwise entertaining her poorly potty-trained schnauzer, Bruno, a job that called for him to carry a copy of her key.

"She has an antique wooden captain's chair with open arms that would be perfect for Diane Sawyer," said Frank. "It has a classic design and simplicity that would help maximize the energy flow in the room. Also, it has a red cushion, which is very good."

Red, according to traditional feng shui interpretation, symbolizes intelligence and clarity.

"It's the space-time balance we're looking for," said Frank.

"I thought we were looking for harmony," said Lois.

"Don't quibble," said Norma.

"But, Frank, we can't just go in and take the chair," I said, which then led me to carefully review for the benefit of all the would-be participants in this heist, Rule Number

Seven on Marcy's Magnificent Seven: "Be bold! But don't take unnecessary risks!" I noted that the criminal code has a name for such behavior. It's called breaking and entering, and it carries a minimum of six years in New York State. No time off for good behavior.

"This isn't worth getting locked up for," I urged. "I don't care if prison stripes *are vertical*."

"I'm the dog-sitter, remember?" said Frank, our very own Johnnie Cochran supplying the defense for burglary. I could practically hear his summation to the jury: "Because I sit, you must acquit."

"Besides," Frank continued, "she'll never know. We'll put the chair back when Diane Sawyer leaves."

"Sounds like a plan," I said, my ethics and caution worn down by Frank's persuasive presentation.

Next thing I knew, Norma, Lois, and I were bickering in whispers, straining under the load of my heavy green living room chair as we slowly made headway to Mrs. Schwartz's apartment. Frank walked ahead of us, keeping on the look-out for nosy neighbors.

We dropped my big chair in Mrs. Schwartz's foyer, and were about to abscond with her elegant wooden one when Lois spotted Bruno, the great watchdog, sleeping soundly on the sofa in the next room. It gave her an inspired idea.

"Let's take him," said Lois.

"Take the dog?" I said, certain I must have heard wrong.

But, alas, I'd heard correctly. On top of offering cookies, Lois thought it would add just the right touch of warmth for me to have Bruno on my lap during the interview.

"Every few minutes, you can pet him," said Lois. "It will be great."

"I don't think so," I said. "For one thing, I'm allergic to dogs."

But Norma and Frank agreed with Lois, and I was too sleep deprived to argue.

Frank awakened Bruno gently, offering him a little doggie treat from Mrs. Schwartz's kitchen. He then scooped up the drowsy schnauzer and carried him back to my apartment. I trailed behind schlepping Mrs. Schwartz's chair, my nose itching from being around dog hairs.

This entire caper took about half an hour. At about 5:45 A.M., once Frank had carefully positioned the stolen chair for maximum karma, all of us collapsed—including Bruno. We each grabbed a nearby piece of floor or sofa and immediately fell sound asleep.

About fifteen minutes later, however, our naps abruptly ended with heavy knocking at my door. Disoriented, I thought at first it must be my neighbor, miniature Mrs. Schwartz, refreshed after the Richard Simmons workout and looking for her missing furniture and dog. But instead, of course, it was Diane Sawyer and her crew. They were right on time. With Frank absent from his post in the lobby, they had come up unannounced.

People who saw the interview are always coming up to me, wanting to know, "What is Diane Sawyer really like?" I'll tell you what I tell them: Much as I try, I have nothing bad to say about her. In person, Diane Sawyer is even blonder and nicer than she seems on television. She is also very tall, which is hard to tell from TV, because a lot of times, she's sitting behind a desk. The one thing I didn't like was her lipstick, which was too dark and too glossy for my taste. In sum, too Monica Lewinsky.

As for the interview itself, the less said the better. It began well enough, in the bathroom of all places, with me showing off Neil's "His" and "Hers" spritzers and pointing to the hole in the plaster where Neil's prized antique Water Pik once stood on a glass shelf.

We then moved to my feng shuied living room, where I pointed out the deep indentation in the rug where Neil's ghastly old dental chair used to be. The grand tour completed, Diane Sawyer settled in Mrs. Schwartz's chair, and I plopped myself across from her on the sofa, right next to Bruno, whom I then slid onto my lap, much as Lois had instructed.

The questions were mainly puffballs about how I felt after getting dumped by Neil on *Filthy Rich!* and my decision to return to the show as a contestant in just three weeks. I fielded these deftly, mostly by repeating answers drilled into my head by Norma. Even as it was happening, I couldn't believe some of militant things tripping off my tongue, but it was just as well because I was too exhausted to have any clear thoughts of my own. At one point, I dutifully held up a copy of Norma's newest book, *Raging Hormones, and Other Outrages,* and urged everyone within the sound of my voice to race out to the bookstore to buy a copy. I felt like a brainwashing victim, but at least things were moving along more or less on an even keel.

It was then that Diane Sawyer turned to the gripping topic of my sex life. Things went rapidly downhill from there.

"I apologize for asking this, but as a serious journalist, I feel I must," she said. "There's been speculation that you and Neil were having trouble in bed, and that was the real reason for your breakup. Is there any truth to that rumor? And, in retrospect, how do you assess Neil as a lover?"

I was startled. Kingman Fenimore hadn't warned me that our deal included me being interrogated about my sex life on national TV at seven-thirty in the morning. I needed time to think. So I reached for Lois's plate of homemade cookies.

"Cookie?" I said. "They're fresh-baked."

"No thank you," said Diane Sawyer. "It's a bit early for me."

Of course, it was also a bit early to be discussing my sex life. If I answered honestly, my guess was it would have people wretching up their breakfasts all over America. But Diane Sawyer did not get to where she is today by shying away from prying questions.

"But back to your sex life with Neil," she persisted. "Any problems there?"

"Well, you know about Neil's obsession with dentistry," I found myself saying. "In bed, he tended to forget I wasn't just another tooth he was drilling."

I regretted those words as soon as I blurted them out. To this day, I kick myself for not answering, "None of your business," and leaving it at that. When you know the camera is running, in theory your instinct should be to carefully censor yourself. But, in fact, the opposite reaction occurs, and you find yourself revealing intensely personal things you haven't even told your girlfriends. You're so concerned with being an interesting "personality" that you forget about everything else. That doesn't excuse my indiscreet answer. But it does help explain why Bill Clinton answered that impertinent question about his taste in underwear early in his presidency, setting a low MTV tone that would permeate two terms. It also explains why "reality TV" bears so little resemblance to reality.

Before Diane Sawyer could serve up a follow-up question, the proceeding was momentarily interrupted by a loud pounding noise. My immediate thought was, Oh no, Mrs. Schwartz is back. But no such luck. It was my mother. Plainly unaware that the whole nation was now privy to her wacky behavior, she was determined to gain entry to her only child's apartment. Right Now!

"It's your mother," she was screaming loud enough to be

picked up on camera. "Let me in. Did you see what that schmuck Neil said about us on *Letterman*? I've retained a lawyer. A nephew of a friend of your uncle Mel. Not a genius like that Alan Dershowitz, but he went to law school near Harvard and he's giving us his family discount rate. We'll go to the Supreme Court if we have to. I know you're not sleeping, Marcy. Let me in."

Finally, after letting my mother go on like that for a while, a bemused Diane Sawyer signaled some stagehands to open the door. Mom swept in right past them only to stop dead in her tracks when she saw the famous newswoman.

"Diane Sawyer!" she said, primping her short silver hair and obviously grateful she had remembered to remove the rollers before leaving her house. "Interviewing my Marcy. I didn't mean to interrupt."

"No interruption. We're glad you came," said Diane Sawyer. "Please join us."

Words are inadequate to convey how much I wished at that moment it had been Mrs. Schwartz at the door instead.

"I watch your show every day," Mom said, joining me on the sofa. "Hi, Charley." She was waving now to Ms. Sawyer's cohost back in the studio, Charles Gibbons.

That was harmless enough. Unfortunately, at some point she stopped waving and turned her attention to me.

"What's this, a dog?" she said, referring to Bruno, who

was now growling ever so faintly at this strange woman who had just plunked herself down next to us. "You don't have a dog. You're allergic."

"I do so, Mom," I said, sneezing. "You must have forgotten." I now addressed myself to Diane Sawyer. "You know, if she doesn't take her gingko—"

"And what about *that*," my mother said, pointing to Mrs. Schwartz's chair. "Where did *that thing* come from? I like your big green chair. Where did it go?"

Trying to stay calm, I took a big breath in and then exhaled, setting off an unfortunate chain reaction that ended the interview. The button on my skirt popped so loudly that it scared poor Bruno half to death. The little schnauzer then hopped off my lap, onto the floor, where he promptly peed on Diane Sawyer's open-toed Manolo Blahniks, apparently mistaking them for the lobby's oriental rug.

The favorite hangout on *Laverne & Shirley* was an establishment owned by Laverne's father, Frank. What was it called?

a. Frank's Italian Eatery
b. The Greasy Spoon
c. Frank's Bar and Grill
d. Pizza Bowl

See correct answer on back. . . .

Thirteen

✦

"You were great with Diane Sawyer. Just great. You're a natural, kid."

It was Kingman Fenimore speaking, and the occasion for sharing this enthusiastic review was a crowded news conference and photo op his people had organized at network headquarters uptown. I was whisked there immediately following my mortifying stint on *Good Morning America* by a hideous white stretch limo with a vinyl leopard-skin roof that looked as if it was borrowed from a pimp. Our chat occurred as Kingman and I posed together atop a hastily erected platform with a giant mock-up of the *Filthy Rich!* logo behind us. Kingman was holding up a much-enlarged $1.75 million check as I looked on approvingly with a big, greedy grin on my face. *Time* and *Newsweek* ran almost identical versions on their covers, only in the superior *Newsweek* version, the dark rings under my eyes were miraculously airbrushed away—a highly appreciated compromise of journalistic ethics that lessened the humiliation of my drab overall appearance.

I didn't have time to change, but my unreliable skirt button was now supplemented by a safety pin for insurance, and a white *Filthy Rich!* T-shirt covered my blue blouse. The shirt had a picture of Kingman on the front, and underneath, his signature phrase was plastered in big red letters: "Absolute Answer?"

"Are we talking about the same show, Kingman?" I said. "Me, my meshuga mother, and the dog with a weak bladder?"

"Yeah, I loved it. Especially the bit with the dog."

I'll have to tell Lois, I thought. Inviting Bruno was her idea. If Kingman liked it, maybe it wasn't so bad after all.

"And your remark about Neil's drilling technique," Kingman continued, "you must have been up all night thinking of that one. It was inspired."

"Ya think? I thought it was pretty embarrassing," I said. " 'Frisky sex vixen' is not the image I'm going for. I'm a Barnard girl."

"You lack perspective," said Kingman. "Being on TV is never having to say you're sorry. Believe me, a few days from now, all people will remember is that they saw you on TV, and they liked you. That's the key in this business. Positive buzz."

"I'll try to remember that," I said. "Positive buzz."

We took just fifteen minutes of questions, which turned out to be fourteen minutes too many, as nearly all the queries sought elaboration on three subjects I didn't wish to discuss: my now-defunct sex life; the name of my secret restaurant companion; and the thorny, still unresolved matter of who I planned to anoint as my Lifeline. I just smiled benignly and kept coming up with creative new ways to say, "No comment." I had exhausted my prepackaged answers from Norma, and I was determined not to run at the mouth like I had with Diane Sawyer. By this time, I'd been up far more than twenty-four hours, and, based on past performance, I had good reason to worry about regrettable things falling from my lips if I let myself get started. Finally, Kingman stepped in and kiddingly lambasted the reporters for showing so little interest in him. "What am I," he asked, feigning insult, "gefilte fish?"

As these festivities were breaking up, Kingman got corraled by a young on-the-make reporter from the *New York Observer*, who was trying to peddle his idea for a new sitcom. The kid looked no more than twenty-three or twenty-four, and sported a J. Press navy blazer and horn-rimmed glasses befitting his air of earnest arrogance and what I surmised was a recent Yale degree.

"I hope you'll consider it, Mr. Fenimore," he said, handing Kingman a large manila envelope. "I've sketched out a few episodes. It's about a big-time game-show host who also does a morning talk show. It could be really funny. And not a big stretch for you acting-wise."

Kingman accepted the envelope and tucked it under his right arm. "A game-show host who also does a morning show," he repeated, politely wending his way around to a gentle rejection that succeeded in deflecting the immediate request without being abrupt or dismissive.

"It has real potential, I think," said Kingman. "Very original. I'll have my agent look at it but, to be realistic, I just don't see having the time. If I were you, I'd change it to the sitcom adventures of a cross-dressing plumber from Hartford, and offer it to that chunky, bearded guy from *The Plank*. He's hot right now, and it would just take some minor retooling. Good luck with it."

"Why were you so nice to that preppy twit?" I asked Kingman once the kid departed.

"He *was* a preppy twit, wasn't he? But he may outgrow it. Who knows, he could turn out to be a TV genius, another Seinfeld. His idea was terrible, I admit, but not so out of line with the crap that sells these days. Maybe when I'm feeble and forgotten, in another two hundred years or so, he'll give me a guest shot."

"I don't see it," I said. "I think you just wasted some of your legendary niceness on the wrong guy."

" 'The wrong guy'?" teased Kingman. "Well, maybe I should listen, then. You have plenty of expertise when it comes to picking the wrong guy."

As we started walking out together, Kingman took a quick look at his $2,500 Raymond Weil watch. I wasn't sure my father's dead-roach count even went that high.

"Well, it's about my lunchtime," Kingman announced.

Then he turned to me. "How about it, Marcy?" he said. "Have you eaten?"

"Not today, yet, but for the past three days, Kingman, thanks to your game show, I've done nothing *but* eat," I said. "It's why I have a safety pin holding my skirt together."

"Marcy Lee," Kingman said with mock exasperation, "I said I was hungry. I didn't mean to open up a conversation about your safety pin. It's not enough that Tracy Ellen took up most of the morning show sharing the ups and downs of her ongoing zits problem? A man can take only so much."

"My safety pin and I apologize," I said.

"Good. Now how about grabbing some lunch? I'm under strict orders from my wife to eat before going home. She says our thirty-two-year marriage won't survive if I insist on being underfoot the entire day."

"Sure," I said, flattered by the invitation from one of the nation's most popular TV personalities. "Where to?"

"Leave it to me," said Kingman.

Put aside thoughts of a celebrity hangout like the Russian Tea Room, or even an ordinary coffee shop with tables, chairs, and central heating. Our first stop after leaving the news conference was Gray's Papaya, the tiny hot-dog emporium at Broadway and Seventy-second Street, which many frankfurter devotees, including Kingman Fenimore, consider a holy shrine—a veritable Lourdes, if you will, for those whose spiritual desires run to fatty smoked sausage, flavor-fully seasoned and grilled to perfection with a crisp outside and then unceremoniously plopped in a soft, white bun.

At least that's how Kingman described the religious experience called Gray's Papaya as we waited in his Town Car while his driver picked up a half dozen of its nitrate marvels for the surprise lunch-hour "picnic" Kingman sprang on me.

"You're in for a real treat," he promised, as we watched with heavy anticipation through the Town Car window as his driver paid the cashier for the hot dogs, all of which were smeared with mustard and buried under a heavy blanket of sauerkraut and spicy cooked onions, as per Kingman's instructions, before getting packed inside little Styrofoam boxes to keep them warm. The order came with two huge cups of sugary orange drink, which Kingman and I sipped as we headed in lighter than usual midday traffic toward the next stop—the New York Waterway terminal at Thirty-eighth Street and the Hudson River.

We arrived just in time to board the nearly empty noon ferry to Weehawken, something Kingman explained he tries to do at least once a week to get a break from the day-to-day pressures of show business and his own newly ballooned celebrity.

"Isn't this great?" he enthused as we planted ourselves at a little round table inside the small vessel's glassed-in cabin. "There are hardly any passengers this time of day, and they generally leave me alone. No one screams, 'Is that your absolute answer,' every time I yawn, as if I'd never heard the joke before. The crew lets me stay onboard for a few round-trips without debarking, so I always leave feeling refreshed, like I just took a mini-vacation cruise on one of those fancy ocean liners Tracy Ellen gets paid a bundle to endorse."

The view crossing was incredible, stretching from the George Washington Bridge to the Statue of Liberty and beyond, and taking in Manhattan's glistening midtown sky-line, New Jersey's Hudson waterfront, and the southern end of the Palisades.

"I lived my first ten years in Weehawken," Kingman reminisced between bites of hot dog and sips of orange drink, "so when the ferry heads in this direction, I feel as if I'm returning to my roots. My father was a bricklayer. Not a bricklayer like you see today. He was a real artist, and he loved his work. We had a house in the little Irish-Italian neighborhood that preceded that giant high-rise over there. For my father, it had to be a brick house, but since he didn't build it himself, he was always finding faults in the work-manship. My mother always said he would have been a lot happier with wood shingles, and she was right. When I was eleven, my parents decided they wanted to raise their five kids in the country. So they sold the Weehawken place and bought a nearly identical house in a nearly identical ethnic neighborhood in Queens, which, believe it or not, still had farmland left. But we hardly ever got near it, since the so-called country was miles from the place my parents went to all that trouble to relocate us to. Go figure."

By now, Kingman had wolfed down two frankfurters and was plowing through his third. "Ready for your second yet, Marcy?"

"Nope, I think I'm set," I said. "My stomach is still in rebellion over the first. I think it may secede later."

In all, we did three round-trips across the river, a forty-five-minute-plus respite that proved every bit as enjoyable as Kingman had promised, although not because of the hot dogs, which I could have done without, or even the striking views from the water of both shorelines. What made it special was getting to spend time with Kingman, who in person turned out to be pretty much the same charming and funny eccentric viewers see on TV, only more endearing.

"See way up there," Kingman said, pointing to a high cliff as we departed Weehawken for our third and final time. "There's a little green up there where Aaron Burr and Alexander Hamilton had their famous duel. The outcome wasn't pretty, and Mr. Hamilton, one of the country's great statesmen, ended up losing his life. But I give both men this much: They were acting as gentlemen, which is more than I can say about your ex-boyfriend Neil."

At that Kingman turned his head from Weehawken and looked directly at me.

"Marcy, whatever happens in the next three weeks, whether you end up winning our jackpot or not," he said,

"I want you to know that you're already a *Filthy Rich!* winner in my book. Maybe the biggest. Just for getting rid of that guy. Try to remember that."

I thanked Kingman, and told him he sounded a lot like my exterminator father. " 'It's crazy,' Dad told my mother when she got home from the show. 'I spend my whole life killing roaches, and my daughter would have ended up marrying one if it wasn't for *Filthy Rich!* ' "

The one remaining thing on my schedule following the ferry ride was a drop-in at the midtown studio of a competing network to make a cameo appearance on the long-running soap opera *Days of Our Lives*. I was assigned to play a dedicated psychiatrist, Dr. Doris Lundgren. The specially written part called for me to don hospital whites and offer uplifting spiritual counsel to a young woman rendered suicidal by the news that her boyfriend blew the big cash prize on a major nighttime quiz show, and they would not be millionaires after all.

I had only two lines. Or just one line, depending on how you count these things. "Don't worry," I solemnly intoned, reading the pithy dialogue off cue cards. "There will be other quiz shows."

Leaving the studio, I asked one of the young scriptwriters why they opted to have my Dr. Lundgren character serve as an enabler, encouraging her patient's unhealthy game-show fantasy instead of helping her realize that money isn't everything. "It's not believable," he said, plainly taken aback by my inquiry. "We try to keep it real."

❧

At this point, I was not traveling alone. From the news conference forward, I was shadowed by two burly private security officers, Abdoul and Waldo, who were hired by the *Filthy Rich!* production office to keep away overly enthusiastic fans and to make sure I adhered to the daily schedule of appearances dictated by the show's chief publicist, a seasoned pro named Maxine Ferris, who generally arrived at events before I did to coordinate any press interviews and otherwise help make things run smoothly.

My two bodyguards were very big, and their dark, shiny suits gave them a slightly menacing *Sopranos* look that made them appear even bigger. Disappointingly, their bigness didn't extend to being big conversationalists; their combined daily word output wouldn't fill a whole minute on *The View*. Also, Abdoul was married, and Waldo had a girlfriend, which was sort of a downer for Lois.

Kingman was genuinely fond of me, I felt. But I knew the decision to sic Abdoul and Waldo on me for protection was nothing personal. I was valuable property, and this was an inexpensive investment to make sure I arrived at the *Filthy Rich!* showdown properly promoted and in one piece.

❧

After returning home from my soap-opera debut, I laid down on the sofa and dozed for a while. I would have been much more comfortable in my bed, and likely would have slept right through the night. Instead, I woke up a little before 7 P.M., sneezing from Bruno's leftover dog hairs and with a painful crick in my neck owing to a bad combination of tension and the sofa's lack of any real support, which is not to disparage Lois's generosity in giving it to me.

Hungry, I called up and ordered a small pizza, taking pains to explain that I wanted just sauce on the pie—no cheese. I wasn't sure if, technically, what I ordered should even be called a "pizza," as cheese would seem a defining ingredient, but I was impressed by my returning dietary restraint. Marcy's Magnificent Seven were definitely back in play. I was proud to be shunning fattening foods (Rule Number Two), and I almost couldn't wait for bedtime, when I would take care to floss (Rule Number One), and moisturize (Rule Number Four).

While waiting for my dinner delivery, I instinctively turned on the TV, happening to hit *E! News Daily* just as the influential cable entertainment show was beginning a report on the results of a new national poll, taken in the immediate aftermath of my talk with Diane Sawyer. It showed me pulling even with Eleanor Roosevelt on the list of women Americans most admire, and actually besting FDR's wife among women ages thirty-five and under. Wow! I thought, this is what Kingman was talking about— the power of positive buzz. But I still had enough self-awareness to know that, unlike Mrs. Roosevelt, I had done nothing whatsoever to merit my new popularity. After all, the former First Lady served as her husband's eyes and legs, visiting the coal miners and troops overseas. I don't think I ever met a real coal miner, and the only troops I have contact with are the Girl Scouts who sell me cookies each year, which I promptly give to my doorman Frank lest I end up single-handedly devouring all dozen boxes of those addictive Thin Mints.

In fact, the more I compared my résumé with Mrs. Roosevelt's, the more I came up short. She stood up against bigotry, for goodness sake, resigning her membership in the DAR when it barred the great black contralto Marian Anderson from singing in Constitution Hall. She wrote a widely read daily newspaper column, and, in her later years, helped found the United Nations. Getting dumped by your boyfriend on TV seemed a puny achievement alongside that. Still, I think *The New York Times* editorial page went too far a few days later when it railed that my high standing in the national poll was "a sad embodiment of a downward cultural slide."

That Howell Raines, who runs the editorial page, is "one smart cookie," according to my mother, the discussion leader a few years back when her ladies' reading club took up the recipes included in his book on fly-fishing. Recalling her admiration for his fish stew only made the pummeling feel worse.

Flipping channels from Eleanor and me, I landed on *Entertainment Tonight*, which was beginning its report on the ongoing real-life drama they were still calling Marcygate.

Since last I'd watched, a mere two nights before, they had created a special logo to introduce their Marcygate stories, using an angry picture of me throwing the ring at Neil. The ever-pert Mary Hart seemed almost gleeful in having a whole litany of "new developments" to share regarding yours truly. She began, unsurprisingly, with my loose-lipped revelation about Neil's approach to lovemaking, in due course segueing to the *Post*'s scoop about my Chinese lunch with an "unidentified" male companion, and then to clips of my news conference with Kingman, and reaction to the announcement that I would soon be appearing as a *Filthy Rich!* contestant. Confirming how big this whole thing was becoming, the president's press secretary indicated that the nation's chief executive might postpone a foreign trip to tune in. I assumed he was joking.

Here I got up to go to the john, figuring I had survived this episode of Marcygate more or less intact. However, I was stopped dead in my tracks by the picture suddenly flashed on the screen.

"And Marcy's not the only one stepping out with some-one new," Mary Hart informed viewers. "This photo, taken exclusively for *Entertainment Tonight* at a benefit last night for the NYU dental school, shows Marcy's ex, Neil Postit, whispering in the ear of the new mystery woman he escorted to the fashionable soiree."

That's no "mystery woman," I said to myself. That's the Burger Queen/Bandanna Lady—my soon-to-be-former client Jane McDee. In the photo, she wasn't wearing any head wear and you could clearly see her dark roots poking through her phony blondness. But she looked a lot happier than I was feeling at that particular moment. Neil may be quirky, even odd. But as the photo reminded me, my six-foot ex is also a pretty attractive guy, especially in a tux. I took off my right slipper and threw it at the screen. Hard.

Knowledge is supposed to be power. But seeing this visual evidence of Neil's apparent two-timing was a decidedly mixed blessing. From a purely professional standpoint, I was glad to finally have an explanation as to why it was taking so long to treat Jane McDee's buck teeth. But obtaining that explanation caused me to relapse into depression. Romance-wise, Neil seemed in great shape, especially if your taste runs to dumb heiresses with bad hair. No looking back for him. Me, I was waxing nostalgic over the good times with Neil—and yes, to be honest, there were good times—and waiting for Cliff Jentzen to get off his lazy butt and give me a call.

I immediately reached for the phone, but it wasn't to call Norma to concede that she'd been right all along about Neil. Nor was it to call my "mystery man," Cliff.

No, I picked up the phone to call the pizza place.

"The Mallowitz order hasn't gone out yet? Great," I said. "Remember the small pizza I ordered, hold the cheese? I was just kidding. Change that to a large pie with extra cheese. And could you toss on some sausage while you're at it?"

Which of these TV celebrities has yet to make an exercise or diet video?

a. Heather Locklear
b. Matt Lauer
c. Suzanne Somers
d. Regis Philbin

See correct answer on back. . . .

ANSWER

✦

b. Matt Lauer

Fourteen

◆

I had a vivid dream that Oprah Winfrey was beating me with a large, empty pizza box. Crumbs were bouncing onto the blanket, and she was yelling at me to get out of bed, and stop the pigging out already.

In all candor, this was not the first dream I'd had like this. In the Old Days—meaning my pre–*Filthy Rich!* days—I often had such dreams. I never saw a doctor about them. I just chalked them up as God's little punishment for my skipping kick-boxing class to go out to lunch with Lois or Norma.

This time, however, it was no guilt-induced hallucination. This time, it really was Oprah. In my bedroom. In person.

When I finally opened my eyes, America's talk-show goddess was standing over me. She stepped back when she saw I was awake. The clock on my night table said 6:00 A.M.

"Oprah?" I said, reaching out to touch her arm. "This isn't a dream this time, is it?"

"No, Marcy," said Oprah. "This is no dream. And look who I brought."

I no longer had a boyfriend, but my bedroom was hardly empty.

Standing just to Oprah's right was her Personal Life Coaching guru, Dr. Phil, whom she had wisely brought along to work on my sagging motivation.

"Hi, Marcy," he said, wasting no time. "We're all here to help you. But first you've got to want to help yourself. Are you ready to do that now, or are you just going to keep wallowing in late-night sausage pizzas? It's your decision."

"I'm ready," I said, exuding impressive confidence for someone newly roused from a deep slumber and feeling cold and overexposed in skimpy pj's. That Dr. Phil, I thought, he's awesome. I'd eaten the whole pie. How could he know it was a *sausage* pizza?

Standing to Oprah's other side were Lois and Norma, seeming uncommonly peppy for the early hour, especially considering our recent all-night cleanup for Diane Sawyer. The two were jogging in place, adorned in fancy exercise outfits from Oprah that called to mind fruit smoothie hour at the Equinox juice bar—especially the sweat bands, which were carefully dyed to match the stripe on their skintight Lycra warm-up pants. I was impressed. Somehow Lois and Norma managed to smile and wave at me without breaking stride.

Beyond this grouping, I now noticed, were two large television cameras capturing this heartwarming tableau on videotape.

"Cut," said Oprah, calling for a halt in the filming.

Oprah explained that she planned to devote a segment of her show each day to an up-close-and-personal report on my progress getting ready for my *Filthy Rich!* showdown.

"Like a mini-documentary," I said.

"Think of it as your own daily 'reality' show," said Oprah.

"Like *The Plank*?" I said.

"Better than *The Plank*," said Oprah. "You get to sleep at home, and you don't have to eat rats."

"Kingman says the rats are from Spago."

"Gourmet rats," said Oprah, bemused. "Maybe I should include them in my next healthy-living cookbook. We'll call it 'gourmet vermin' so it sounds like a French dish."

The conversation turned to Oprah's thick new glossy magazine, *O*. Maybe it was a tad presumptuous on my part, but I couldn't resist saying I thought the eighteen pictures of her in the last issue weren't nearly enough. I also told her I thought she should consider giving Dr. Phil's column more prominence, and that *O*'s recent profile of a young Manhattan woman who sold her extensive designer shoe collection to pay for her mother's fiftieth-birthday spiritual pilgrimage to Tibet was so moving, it made me cry.

Oprah excused herself to consult with Dr. Phil and a harried young woman around my age who later introduced herself as Oprah's producer. She soon returned to brief me. "We'll open the first segment with the bedroom scene we just shot," she said. "After you get dressed, Marcy, I want to follow with a shot of me leading you and your friends on a jog around a park. What's nearby?"

"Washington Square Park is only three blocks down," I said. "It's usually pretty deserted this time of day. We can run around the perimeter." I warned that we might be joined by a few of the drug dealers who continue to own the park's southeast corner.

"I love it," said Oprah, tossing me a new jogging suit similar to the exotic numbers my friends were already wearing. "There's nothing like urban flavor."

So off we trotted. In the beginning, our group consisted of Oprah, followed just a few steps behind by Norma and me, with Lois and my hulking dark-suited bodyguards, Abdoul and Waldo, dragging up the rear. But by the end of two laps, our pack had grown to several dozen, as people recognized Oprah, and then me, and decided they wanted to be part of history in the making. The action was captured by Oprah's camera crew from the rear of a small flatbed truck, which rolled along inconspicuously slightly ahead of us. When Oprah aired the tape on her show, she added the music from *Chariots of Fire*, and played the last few minutes in slow motion. An inspired touch, I thought.

After our jog, Oprah took me to a park bench to fire me up for the task ahead. We were joined by Dr. Phil, who had somehow managed to get exempted from our little run.

"What is it now, almost three weeks until the show?" Oprah said. "The pressure is going to be incredible, Marcy, and you need to be prepared, mentally, physically, and spiritually. I'm going back to Chicago, but we'll be checking on your progress every day on my show. I want to see you and your friends out here jogging first thing every morning. We need your endorphins flowing."

"Oprah's right on," added Dr. Phil. "We're here because we believe in you, Marcy. But what counts is, you've got to believe in yourself. Have some self-respect. You call yourself a Personal Life Coach? You want others to respect you? Stop behaving like a loser and show us your stuff."

"Cut," ordered Oprah.

The visit by Oprah and Dr. Phil was a real wake-up call. The whole nation was watching. I needed to shape up—and quickly.

Life is strange, I thought. A week ago who could have predicted the biggest challenge of my Personal Life Coaching career would turn out to be me?

In one hilarious *I Love Lucy* episode, Lucy comes up with the "million-dollar idea" of making a TV commercial with Ethel touting the virtues of what product?

a. Aunt Martha's Salad Dressing
b. Ricky Ricardo's new album
c. Vitameatavegamin
d. Fresh eggs from Lucy's chickens in Connecticut

See correct answer on back. . . .

Fifteen

◆

The next weeks passed by in a blur. As followers of her show can attest, the intervention by Oprah and Dr. Phil brought immediate and dramatic results. I morphed into a model of discipline, getting to bed by nine each evening and awakening around five each morning to the sound of my little novelty alarm clock playing reveille. After five minutes of stretching exercises, I would dutifully down the vile protein shake Oprah insisted would be my salvation, along with a bulging cellophane packet containing what I imagined to be every vitamin and mineral known to man. The combination induced an uncomfortable sensation of nausea that lasted much of the morning, but it was worth it. When I wasn't feeling sick to my stomach, it gave me a special feeling of confidence to know I had met or exceeded the daily minimum requirement in every vital category.

I get a lot of letters from people asking, "What's your secret, Marcy? How did you maintain your superhuman level of motivation for the whole three weeks preceding your return to *Filthy Rich!*? My New Year's resolutions seem to fade by New Year's Day brunch."

It's a good question, and thanks for sharing. First of all, I drew a lot on my personal faith. I'm a big believer that every painful experience contains an important opportunity for personal growth, and not just in the sense of larding on unneeded pounds searching for emotional solace in a dozen boxes of chocolate-covered Mallomars, which, of course, I've done, too. Also remember, unlike most of you slackers, I went into my *Filthy Rich!* training with years of experience as a Personal Life Coach, which allowed me to draw on techniques I've seen work well for my coaching clients.

Take my motivational signs, for example. Like many women, I have a tendency to lapse into depression when little things in life go wrong, like the man you thought you'd marry dumps you like so much smelly garbage on national TV. To help keep me energized and positive, I printed motivational messages on rectangular pieces of cardboard using a blue Flair pen, and hung them all over my apartment. My doorman Frank obtained the cardboard for me by raiding the building's returning shirt packages from the dry cleaners. But if your home doesn't have a doorman, or you feel you can't ask a favor since you chintzed on the last Christmas gift, regular sheets of paper will also do just fine. Until you try this method yourself, you can have no idea how heartening it was to see a "Go, Marcy, Go!" sign first thing as I stepped out of the shower. Another useful sign, which I Scotch-taped to the back of my apartment door, listed

Marcy's Magnificent Seven, and provided room to check off which of its wise rules I'd lived up to each day. Framed and autographed by yours truly, the completed chart fetched $3,000 when it was auctioned off recently to benefit that children's project in the Bronx that Ellewina and I visited together just before she died.

I'm such a sucker for signs, I even taped one to my bedroom ceiling, which turned out to be a big mistake because the message I chose—that dependable old fave, "Quitters Never Win, Winners Never Quit"—was a misfit. It was good for waking up in the morning, but not for helping someone running on twenty tons of mystery supplements calm down enough to fall asleep.

But sleep deprived or not, promptly at six each morning, I'd meet Lois and Norma downstairs in my lobby for our daily jog. As *Filthy Rich!* loomed closer, the crowd running with us continued to grow, and so did our route. Instead of simply circling the small park twice, and jogging back to my apartment building at Tenth Street and Fifth Avenue, we'd circle three times, and then run past my building, venturing a few blocks farther up Fifth Avenue each day. In addition to Abdoul and Waldo, the mayor assigned me a police escort, which came in handy to control the traffic as we moved up the avenue en masse, accompanied by innumerable camera vans beyond the one for Oprah's Marcy Lee Mallowitz reality project, some with huge satellites mounted on top.

This amazing display of support had me pumped. But

some mornings, as I glanced behind at our pack of joggers, I couldn't help but feel a little embarrassed by all the populist energy being expended for a cause no greater than my pursuit of Kingman Fenimore's $1.75 million prize. I silently vowed to myself that if I won the money, I would give a sizable portion to charity. Cynical media types may question my sincerity. I can live with that. It grates less than Joan Rivers's likening my thighs to "two colliding tugboats caught in a Jell-O spill," as she did on her much-touted cable fashion special dedicated to reviewing our jogging suits. To think I used to count myself a big fan of Joan's almost single-handed effort to elevate Hollywood couture.

And speaking of jogging suits, Lois and Norma stuck by my side the whole way, putting their own social and professional lives on hold to help me meet my *Filthy Rich!* challenge. I only hope it was as positive an experience for my friends as it was for me, despite Joan's bitchiness about our fabulous outfits.

Another question I get a lot concerns my stamina. I've received lots of letters from people who are amazed I could do the jogging, and all the other publicity things piled on my plate the week before my Big Broadcast, and still manage to prepare for Kingman's questions. "Marcy, are you superwoman, or what?" they want to know.

I'm no superwoman, but the reason it sometimes appears that way has to do with my super powers in one area: I'm a fantastic organizer, having started my Life Coaching career in the closet-renewal game. The key was to make good use of odd corners of the day, just as I taught clients to make good use of odd corners of their closets.

Once back at my apartment after jogging, Lois, Norma, and I would take turns in the shower. After getting dressed, we'd get down to the important business of studying, with my two school chums tossing questions at me in rapid-fire order, drawn from the vast array of magazines, world almanacs and atlases, science texts, and movie books we amassed in short order in my living room—a veritable library of arcane trivia and useless factoids. It was like the old days when the three of us would prepare together for finals, only in college, you more or less knew the subject matter of the test you were studying for. Not so on *Filthy Rich!*, where questions skidded unpredictably across the whole range of human knowledge. We figured the best we could do was to stuff my brain indiscriminately until it was near bursting, and then hope and pray the people who think up the questions would go light on geography, math, and anything having to do with weight lifting, wrestling, or my well-known nemesis, TV variety shows.

So intense was this quest for knowledge, my friends persisted in prodding me with questions even during lunch.

"First American woman in space," Lois would say, grabbing for some kosher pickle slices to top off her turkey on whole wheat.

"Sally Field," I'd answer between bites of my tuna salad with celery and fat-free mayo.

"Wrong Sally, but close. She's the flying nun," Norma would correct me between slugs of Diet Coke.

I'd try again. "Sally Hemings."

"You're getting colder. She slept with Thomas Jefferson and she wasn't even airborne. Our Sally rhymes with lied, as in 'Neil lied to you about being faithful.' "

"Sally Ride." Having finally gotten it right, there'd be high fives all around, but no pause in the questioning.

"Best picture, 1995?"

"Who says?"

"The Academy."

"Easy, *Braveheart*. But *Ed Wood* was robbed. I'd take Johnny Depp over Mel Gibson any day." We high-fived with gusto on that one.

These sessions would go on like this for hours, although sometimes we had to conduct them crammed into the backseat of a limo on the way to one of my many media appearances. One of the most gratifying was my star turn on Rosie O'Donnell's morning show. I went on dressed in the pink sweatsuit she had sent me, freshly washed, and was able to tell "the Queen of Nice" in person how comforting it was to wear it during the first dark days post–Neil Postit. I also thanked her for the Ding Dongs, while explaining that I was back on the wagon where fattening junk food was concerned, and grew misty-eyed imploring her to renew her contract to do the show when it runs out in 2002. "America needs you, Rosie," I said.

Rosie loves Broadway, and so do I, so she had the two of

us sing a song from *Fiddler on the Roof*, with its lyrics slightly altered to fit my situation. "If I were a rich girl," the two of us warbled. I thought we sounded pretty good.

Another high point was the filming of my first paid television commercial. I resent it when celebrities lend their endorsement to worthless products they know are crappy and overpriced, and would never allow into their own home. But I felt proud to be the one chosen to introduce viewers to Fritzies, an exciting breakthrough in fat-free snack crackers, tasty enough to be named "The Official Snack Cracker of the 2002 Olympics."

One good thing about my busy schedule was that it didn't allow me much time to dwell on Neil's departure, or the apparent disappearance of my promising new hopeful, Cliff Jentzen. It had been refreshing talking to a straight, single guy who actually seemed to be interested in what I was thinking and feeling. Well, probably not that interested, I decided on second thought, since he hadn't bothered to call.

Never far from my thinking, meanwhile, was the still-unresolved issue of who I would choose for my Lifeline. My first choice would have been Kingman, but he was off-limits for obvious reasons. Someone suggested Florida's Republican secretary of state, Katherine Harris. I don't know her personally. But she obviously has solid Lifeline experience, having served in that capacity for George W. Bush when she prematurely certified her state's presidential election results. Rosie volunteered to be my Lifeline when I appeared on her show, and I was tempted to accept. She's a big *Filthy Rich!* fan. But a tiny voice inside me—Ellewina's, I imagine—told me, "Not so fast. Your Lifeline Destiny lies elsewhere."

Truth is, I had secretly decided I would draft my mother as my Lifeline if no more obvious choice emerged by the night before my triumphant return to *Filthy Rich!* when I was scheduled to appear on *Larry King Live*. As Lifelines go, I could do a lot worse. Mom's no great intellectual. But she's a charter subscriber to *People* who's read everything by Mary Higgins Clark and never misses the "Can This Marriage Be Saved?" feature in *Ladies' Home Journal*. And if Kingman tossed out any kugel questions, I figured I'd be set.

Up until the very last minute, it looked like Mom would be It. But then, sitting there with Larry King, something startling happened to change my mind. Toward the end of the program, when my host opened the phone lines for questions, the first caller turned out to be someone I knew very well—my ex, Neil. That's right, lousy, lying, strangely compelling Neil Postit, D.D.S. He said he wanted me back, and to prove it, he was volunteering to be my Lifeline.

For the second time in less than three weeks, he'd ambushed me on live national television, except this time at least, it was cable, and he was trying to be nice. Or so it seemed.

"That picture of me whispering in Jane McDee's ear," he said, "it's not what you think."

"Really," I said. "Are you saying it was trick photography? A doctored shot from the mysterious grassy knoll?"

"I'm serious, Marcy," he said. "The band was really loud, so I was talking directly into her ear. I told her to take two aspirins. Her braces were cutting into her gums."

"So what you're saying, Neil, if I understand it, is you're sorry for your behavior, and you want back with Marcy here," said Larry King, summing up.

"That's right, Larry. I made a mistake exploding like I did after I lost on *Filthy Rich!* But I still love Marcy. And I hope she'll let me be her Lifeline tomorrow night. I practiced a lot when I was trying out to be a contestant, and together we'd be a great team. That's what I want if Marcy will have me: to be a team again. To spritz together. Marcy will get what I mean."

Larry could barely contain his excitement at having this scoop fall into his lap. "Wow!" he said. "Viewers, I want you to know we did not prearrange this. We're as stunned as you are. Marcy, what do you say to Neil?"

Frankly, I didn't know what to say. Was Neal returning because he really missed me or because I was now a hot media babe with lots of positive buzz and lucrative endorsement deals? And what about me? Did I really want Neil back, or was the breakup really a blessing in disguise, freeing me from a prosaic lifetime of courtesy tooth cleanings and orthodontic anecdotes, just as Kingman had said? On the other hand, Neil sounded sweetly repentant, even if I didn't buy for a nanosecond the fairy tale about him and the Burger Queen/Bandanna Lady, Jane. I felt my lips start to move, but I wasn't sure what would spill out.

"Yes," I said.

"Yes?" said Larry King. "Yes, what?"

"Yes, Neil can be my Lifeline," I said. "That's as far as I can think right now. We'll see what happens tomorrow night."

"Hear that, Neil?" said Larry. "You're a go for Marcy's Lifeline, and the two of you can take it from there. I feel romance in the air. Good luck to both of you on *Filthy Rich!* tomorrow night. It's another network. But it's a bet we'll all be watching. The news is next."

Norma was so peeved when I took Neil as my Lifeline that she almost didn't show up for our final jog before *Filthy Rich!* It was as if in doing so, I had personally betrayed her, Gloria Steinem, Murphy Brown, and every other dedicated feminist going back to Susan B. Anthony.

"Why did you do it, Marcy?" Norma asked when I met her and Lois in my lobby at 6 A.M. that morning.

"I'm not sure," I said. "Everything's happened so fast. Maybe I just didn't want to disappoint Larry King. He seemed awfully happy I said yes to Neil on his show." What I was thinking, but didn't say, was that I wished it had been Cliff who called me on Larry King.

"Well, that's some progress," said Norma, softening. "At least you didn't try to blame it on Marcia Brady."

For all this swirling confusion, I felt strangely calm. That cheery little voice inside was telling me to relax. It would all work out for the best.

"Let's get jogging," said Lois. "Our public is waiting."

The crowd that last morning was at least double the size of the day before, ballooned in part by people who had flown in from around the country to send me off to *Filthy Rich!* in style. Lois, Norma, and I were so psyched by our following that we ended up jogging a lot farther up Fifth Avenue than we had planned, going all the way to Forty-second Street, and the main branch of the New York Public Library. As the crowd waited below, cheering, my two girlfriends and I ran up the library's formidable steps, triumphantly pumping the air with our fists when we reached the top.

When Oprah played a videotape of the scene on her show later that morning, keying it to the theme music from the movie *Rocky*, the entire studio audience spontaneously rose to its feet and applauded hard for a full three minutes. In the wings, so did Dr. Phil.

I was ready.

An era sadly ended when original *Brady Bunch* cast member Maureen McCormick did not return to portray Marcia Brady in one of the show's TV spinoffs. The family still got together, but for true Marcia fans, the magic was gone. Which spinoff was it?

a. *A Very Brady Christmas*
b. *The Brady Bunch Hour*
c. *The Bradys*
d. *The Brady Brides*

See correct answer on back. . . .

ANSWER

✦

c. The Bradys

Sixteen

✦

"Tonight. Live. Marcy Lee Mallowitz returns to play for $1.75 million on a special edition of *So You Want to Be Filthy Rich!"* Even as the show's announcer screamed those words, it was hard for me to believe this was really happening.

To think only a couple of weeks before I'd entered this same studio on Neil's arm, a semi-successful Personal Life Coach with a bad haircut, virtually unknown outside my own little circle of family, friends, and rich, self-absorbed clients. I was returning a certified national celebrity—I'd sung Broadway with Rosie, for goodness sake, become pals with Larry King and Oprah, and thanks to my commercial endorsement, Fritzies were well on their way to becoming a staple of the American diet. When I arrived at the studio this second time—separately from Neil—Kingman Fenimore himself came out to greet me. As cameras flashed away, we confidently waved and flashed thumbs-up signs to the large, enthusiastic crowd that had begun gathering on the sidewalk outside the studio hours before my arrival to catch a glimpse of yours truly.

I wore the same drop-dead black column gown from Armani I'd seen Ashley Judd wear to a glitzy movie premiere covered by *E!* My hair, for once, was cooperating with my attempt at a casually sexy Jennifer Aniston look, although that cooperation broke down somewhat when my *former* stylist, the great Giovanni, showed up uninvited backstage begging forgiveness in that suave Italian accent of his, and I let him make a few minor adjustments with a styling brush just for old times' sake.

Still, in all, I thought I looked pretty terrific—a far, far cry from my brief but pathetic binge period.

"You look a lot better," said Kingman, proud and relieved that his gamble on the bedraggled female he'd picked up on East Tenth Street three weeks ago had paid off. I took it as a compliment.

I only wished my father had agreed to come. But he said he'd be too nervous, and besides, he never wanted to be in the same room with Neil again. That's my dad, I thought. I felt for the unique pendant he'd given me as a Hanukkah gift when I was four and adored nothing more than to accompany him on his weekend jobs—an Egyptian scarab he'd had a jeweler friend encase in a thin, round piece of clear Plexiglas and then string on a delicate silver chain as a token of those great times together. Holding it gently between my fingers, my mind latched on to a mental picture of myself as a little girl, excitedly unwrapping the small box containing Dad's special present.

"Do you like it?" he'd asked nervously as I picked it up for inspection. *Like it? Was he kidding?* "I love it, Daddy," I screamed, running into his arms. I can still feel his hug. I feel it every time I put on Dad's sweet if slightly scary lucky charm.

This pleasant flashback was abruptly dissolved by the voice of my mother, whose otherwise sentimental nature has never warmed to Dad's kooky concept of dead-roach jewelry.

"I can't believe you're still wearing that grotesque thing," she said upon spotting it hanging from my neck. "I love your father dearly, but his taste sometimes is from hunger. At least tuck it inside your dress so Kingman doesn't get rattled during the game and call in a fumigator."

I didn't know it at the time, but the evening's ratings battle was already won. The producers of *The Plank,* the competition whose sky-high ratings caused Kingman to desperately seek this return appearance, chickened out at the last minute from competing toe to toe with our extravaganza. They canceled the weekly hour with the Burbank castaways on the flimsy pretext that everyone connected with the cheesy endeavor was suffering severe intestinal pains due to a glitch involving the seasoning for the Spago rats.

Realistically, however, this was just a temporary victory in a larger war. *The Plank* would be coming back the next week, and, according to the papers, casting was already under way for *The Plank II*, featuring a whole new set of castaways and the added twist of special guest stars every week. Yet more "reality" shows were on the horizon, including a provocative new hidden camera series from Fox called *Pardon Me* that is rumored to follow Bill Clinton as he hits on different young women each week at the Chappaqua train station. In the months ahead, *Filthy Rich!* would have to come up with more dazzling gimmicks than just Marcy Lee Mallowitz to stay on top. But for the moment, at least, Kingman Fenimore was still TV's king of nighttime "reality," and that wasn't just gefilte fish, as Kingman would say.

⚜

Yes, after all the emotional ups and downs, the jogging and cramming with Norma and Lois, the Big Night had finally arrived.

What an amazing ride, I reflected, waiting backstage to be called out into the *Filthy Rich!* arena, and for the game-show part to actually begin. I wouldn't trade any of it, not even our frenzied feng shui moment before Diane Sawyer's arrival. Well, maybe I'd edit out the part where I meet a great new guy and he doesn't bother to call, leaving me susceptible to Neil's hangdog entreaty on *Larry King Live*.

Neil was allowed to visit briefly backstage to wish me/us

luck. "I love you, Marcy," he said. "Winning tonight is going to bring us back together. You'll see, it's going to be just like it was before."

"Great," I said as pages led Neil back to his seat in the audience—the same seat, fittingly enough, where I'd proved such a flop as his Lifeline. As a precaution against my mother beating Neil bloody with her imitation Louis Vuitton handbag in the event he blew his Lifeline role, or made more rude comments about her pot roast, she was given a prime seat on the opposite side of the set.

Looking up at a monitor backstage, I watched as swirling spotlights and a dramatic drumroll heralded Kingman's entrance, Kingman decked out in his customary dark, monochromatic shirt and tie. The audience thundered as if he was some kind of conquering hero. As he introduced a video of my last disastrous appearance on the show, and highlights of my busy life since, I thought hard about what Neil had said: If we won, it would bring us back together. Things would be just like they were before.

Just like before. Is that really what I wanted? I wasn't sure.

It occurred to me that I sometimes paid more attention to figuring out what Marcia Brady would do in a given situation than what really made sense for Marcy Lee Mallowitz. If it hadn't been for Episode Twenty-five, I wondered, the one where Marcia feigned an interest in insects to snag a bug-obsessed boy on whom she had a crush, would it even have occurred to me to pursue Neil so avidly, reading up on orthodontic issues in boring professional journals so we'd have something to talk about? Beyond our strong physical attraction, and my even stronger desire to get married, what else did we have going?

I tried to refocus my thinking away from this personal muddle. I knew I needed my mind clear if I was going to successfully field Kingman's questions. But I was a Personal Life Coach in turmoil.

If I won with Neil's help, our re-coupling seemed almost inevitable. The public would demand it. For me to stand in the way would seem almost like poor sportsmanship. But a lot had changed since Neil went ballistic three weeks ago and made me the world's most famous dumpee. For one thing, I'd earned enough money plugging products so that the *Filthy Rich!* prize no longer meant as much as it had. My once-strong allergy to the trappings of unearned celebrity could be considered cured. Moreover, I'd learned an important lesson: Just because a couple spritzes together doesn't necessarily mean they fit together.

I'd never missed Ellewina more. My choices wouldn't seem so difficult, I mused, if only my wise old friend were here to advise me.

This reverie ended when I realized my presence was being requested onstage.

"Ladies and gentlemen," Kingman said, "it's time to play *So You Want to Be Filthy Rich!* So let's bring out tonight's special contestant, Marcy Lee Mallowitz!"

Simultaneously, Lois appeared out of nowhere wielding a big, round styling brush. She deftly undid Giovanni's detrimental contribution to my hair with a few quick, last-minute strokes.

"Good luck," said a stagehand.

"Thanks," I said. "I'll need it."

What I was really thinking, in case you're curious, was, I just hope no one calls me a bitch this time.

"For $250,000, Marcy, which White House occupant could appropriately be called 'the bachelor president'? "

I'd made it through the early questions without straining my brain bone. I've never asked Kingman about this, but my hunch is that he and his producers made a deliberate decision to go soft on me in the beginning to ensure that we reached this place of ultimate drama. I was now just three correct answers from the Big Prize.

"James Buchanan," I answered without bothering to hear the other choices. "Absolute answer."

I don't claim any great knowledge about the American presidency. But when man-crazy Lois is your presidential trivia coach, you come away knowing *everyone's* exact marital status, including any cute Secret Service agents'.

The next question, for $500,000, nearly tripped me up.

"For half a million dollars, name the state capital of Alaska," said Kingman. These were the choices:

a. Fairbanks
b. Anchorage

c. Juneau

d. Nome

I'm no great student of the Yukon. Heck, I don't even like the cold. As far as I was concerned, all four cities sounded like they could be the capital. At least I'd heard of them.

Fortunately, I still had all of my help devices left. I asked Kingman to poll the audience. But with no disrespect to audience members, they were as ignorant as I was, splitting their vote evenly among the four choices. Thanks a lot.

Temperatures on the *Filthy Rich!* hot seat can rise mighty quickly, I was learning firsthand, when you don't have the first clue as to which is the right answer. I didn't sweat as much as Neil or Richard Nixon, but, candidly, I think that's only because women tend to have smaller sweat glands. Now why didn't they ask me about *that*? My designer gown would have ended up a lot less soggy.

But back to my Alaska dilemma. When the audience failed me, I decided to try the fifty-fifty option, where they take two incorrect answers away. They left just these two choices remaining:

a. Fairbanks

c. Juneau

At first, this winnowing down wasn't much help. Fairbanks and Juneau both sounded capital-worthy to my gullible ears. Then I remembered a little trick Norma had taught me when we reviewed state capitals. At the time, I was pedaling on an exercise bike my doorman Frank had borrowed from the vacationing family in apartment 11-S, and I wasn't paying much attention. But somehow in this moment of desperation, I recalled Norma telling me how to remember Alaska's capital.

"It makes perfect sense," said Norma. "June is warm; Alaska is cold. That's why June no."

"June no," I said. "Absolute answer."

"Juneau it is," said Kingman, "for half a million dollars."

There was then a long commercial break to maximize profits and drama before I got hit with the $1.75 million question. With the blinding TV lights turned down, I had a chance to look around. I spotted Neil and my mother in the audience, and exchanged smiles and waves with both of them. I was trying to make out where Norma and Lois were sitting, but my view of much of the audience was blocked by the giant cameras they had ringing the set with the idea of performing an illusion as impressive as anything David Copperfield has managed—providing quickly shifting angle shots to make what would otherwise be a rather prosaic game show appear ultra-fast-paced. I was admiring the video behemoth straight ahead of me when its operator came out from behind and some missing puzzle pieces started coming together.

The cameraman was my promising Mr. eBay, Cliff Jentzen, who'd been missing in action since he'd taken me out that day for Chinese. So that's how he got my ring, I thought. I'd just assumed when he told me he was in production, he meant deodorants, laundry detergents, and the like. In fairness, he didn't lie. But he wasn't very forthcoming, either.

When he saw he'd gotten my attention, Cliff waved shyly, and mouthed, "Good luck." Much less shyly, I immediately mouthed back, "Where the hell have you been?" But I don't think he saw that. By then, we were back from commercial, the klieg lights were turned back on, and I could no longer see Cliff or his giant camera.

"Well, Marcy, now it's crunch time. Are you ready to go for $1.75 million? Leave now, and you go home with a cool half million. A wrong answer, and your take goes down to $75,000—still not bad for a night's work, but far shy of the $1.75 million prize everyone's rooting for you to win. Your decision?"

"What? Could you please repeat that?" I was totally distracted now, which is not an ideal condition when you're on live TV and have $1.75 million hanging in the balance. Cliff's sudden reappearance had thrown me. Maybe good old Ellewina was trying to give me a sign, I thought. But what did it mean? And what was I supposed to do?

"Well, kid, what will it be? Everyone in the studio audience and at home is waiting on the edges of their chairs. You and Neil got burned once going for the big prize. Are you going to play it safe tonight or try again for the $1.75 million?"

Marcy, concentrate, I told myself. Hold off the identity

crisis just another few minutes. Wait until *after* you've won the $1.75 mil.

"It's a go, Kingman," I said, struggling to get my mind back into the game. "Fire away."

"It's a gusty decision, Marcy. But you're in pretty good shape. You haven't used up all your help options. You still have Neil standing by to be your Lifeline if you need it. Now get ready to play *So You Want to Be Filthy Rich!*"

There was the familiar convulsion of overhead spotlights, and all at once the only sound you could hear was the recording of a pounding heartbeat. I felt my tension level rise accordingly. And there was my hand again, tugging painfully at my hair.

"Marcy, this is a big one," Kingman said, an oasis of calm. "Take your time. And here's the question: On the old *Bob Newhart Show*, which ran from 1972 through 1978, Bob played a Chicago psychologist who shared an office suite with a dentist. For $1.75 million, give us the name of that dentist."

The choices were:

a. George Stoody
b. Jerry Robinson
c. Howard Bordon
d. Dick Loudon

I had to hand it to Kingman and his people, coming up with a final question artfully designed to mix my classic-comedy expertise and early interest in psychology with Neil's obsession with everything dental. As I saw it, Kingman and Co. had intentionally manipulated things to reunite us—as once and future lovers, and as contestant and Lifeline, working in tandem to win the Big Prize. It occurred to me that the inspiration to make the apologetic phone call to Larry King asking to be my Lifeline might not have been Neil's alone. I couldn't help but wonder if Kingman, my newfound ferry friend, had put Neil up to it to enhance his almighty ratings.

"I don't want to screw up like last time," I said. "Before answering, I want to bring Neil in on this."

"That would be Neil Postit, of course, Marcy's Lifeline tonight—a total role reversal from their spat here three weeks ago. There's Neil in our audience. He's an orthodontist for adults, practicing in Manhattan, and he says he's hoping a win tonight will help him and Marcy get back together. Marcy, you and Neil have thirty seconds. Good luck."

What came out of my mouth next surprised everyone, especially me. It was as if a dam had broken, and all of Norma's rants about Neil came flooding forth with my own suppressed litany of hurts and disappointments in one succinct and timely summary.

"Neil," I said, "I can't believe you had the nerve to ask to be my Lifeline after completely humiliating me and insulting my mother's cooking on national television. You only want me back because of the money, and because you want a piece of my celebrity. Well, you can't have it. I'm going to win tonight, but without owing you anything. Bob Newhart is classic comedy, and I know the answer." I paused for breath as Neil sank lower in his chair. "I don't need you as my Lifeline, and I don't need you in my life."

"Marcy, I'm afraid your time is up," said Kingman, acting as if nothing unusual had happened.

"I'm almost done, Kingman," I said. "Just three more words: So long, Neil."

"Way to go, Marcy," I heard Norma yell from somewhere in the audience, igniting a thunderous round of applause that drowned out the show's annoying heartbeat tape.

"Folks, this is what I call a 'reality show,' " said Kingman, obviously pleased by Neil's demise and the prospect that it would generate positive buzz for his show. "You never know what's going to happen." The audience laughed.

"Now that you've gotten that off your chest, Marcy, let's go back to the game," Kingman resumed. "For $1.75 million, we're looking for the name of the dentist on the old *Bob Newhart Show*. You say you know the answer."

"Yes," I said with determination.

"Okay, kid, let's hear it," said Kingman.

"I used to watch the show all the time on *Nick at Night*," I said. "Neil used to tell me he hated the show because everyone laughed at the dentist. I'll say letter *d*, Dick Loudon."

"Absolute answer?" said Kingman.

"Absolute answer."

I have rarely felt as confident of anything in my life. That is, until that awful buzzer noise sounded, signaling that I had blown the money yet again.

A loud collective moan rang out from the audience.

"Sorry, Marcy," said Kingman, seeming authentically pained by the outcome. "We were all rooting for you. But, unfortunately, letter *d*, Dick Loudon, was the name of the how-to book writer Bob Newhart played on his next successful sitcom, *Newhart*, starting in 1982. The dentist in the old show was Jerry Robinson, letter *b*. It's too bad you lost, but . . ."

Kingman couldn't have been more gracious. But I was in no mood to stay and listen. By this time I had left the hot seat, center stage, and was bolting out the nearest door with a red exit sign, somehow navigating the studio's stairs and wires in my Armani gown and high-heeled Jimmy Choos without tripping.

Chaos momentarily reigned in the studio and on screen as Cliff Jenzten spun around his camera while abandoning his assigned perch to run after me, taking a shortcut known only to the crew.

When I emerged into the evening air, I was surprised to find Cliff waiting for me. He was sitting behind the steering wheel of his old Toyota, which he somehow had the foresight to illegally park right outside the studio's back exit for just this eventuality. Its passenger door was open, and Cliff was waving me inside. "We'd better scram if you're serious about getting out of here. I'm sure there's a posse out by now."

The car began moving as soon as I slid into the front seat. "Hungry?" he said.

"Sure I'm hungry," I said. "Losing $1.75 million always leaves me famished. But no dinner plans until you answer me: Why didn't you call? And don't tell me you broke your dialing finger."

"I did try to call, right after our date, but you weren't picking up your phone, and your answering machine was so full it just kept beeping without taking any messages. By the next night, it was too late. You were booked on *Filthy Rich!* and romantic involvement between a guest and staff member is a giant no-no. You seemed to want tonight's shot, and I wasn't going to spoil it for you."

His answer—a pretty good one, I thought—was a conversation stopper. "Oh," I said. "I guess you have a point."

What I was thinking was that my doorman Frank is a pretty good judge of people. He had Cliff pegged right from the start: He's a pretty decent sort.

"I know a place that has great lobster," he said. "Up for it?"

"Sure," I said. "Anything but your Chinese food outpost with the inquiring photographer."

In fact, I haven't eaten a lobster since Mary Tyler Moore's protests made me feel sorry for the little critters. But I thought I'd save that dietary tidbit for a later conversation.

I was just happy to be on the road again with Cliff.

Which celebrity's tenure as host of their own late-night talk show was shortest?

a. Pat Sajak
b. Joey Bishop
c. Joan Rivers
d. Chevy Chase

See correct answer on back. . . .

Seventeen

◆

The great lobster place Cliff had in mind was the state of Maine. We took 95 all the way up there that night, talking the whole time about matters big and small. At the risk of sounding sappy, it was the best eight hours I'd ever spent with a guy who wasn't gay. Around dawn, we stopped for breakfast at a small dive in Portland, and then drove a little farther, finally landing in a tiny town on Lake Sebago, where we rented the cozy waterfront cottage we've called home for the past month as I've been furiously typing away to get this story down.

It's been a wonderful hiatus. In addition to cementing my relationship with Cliff, I also found the perfect spot for that country macramé store my client Dolores Smithers always dreamed about. With some coaching by phone, she's finally ready to make the move. Stop by if you're ever in the neighborhood.

When I've finished writing, which should be any minute

now, Cliff and I will be heading back to our exciting new life together in New York City. In a move that surprised me probably as much as it surprised you, Kingman Fenimore has just tapped me to be the co-host of his morning talk show, replacing his recently departed morning sidekick, the much-beloved Tracy Ellen. Starting tomorrow, it will be *Gabbing! With Kingman and Marcy Lee*. As part of my deal, I've arranged for Norma and Lois to sit in with me whenever Kingman goes on vacation. My mother will appear occasionally to enlighten viewers with her classic Jewish recipes and helpful shopping tips. I hope you tune in. It should be a lot of fun. Tomorrow, by the way, I also start private acting and singing lessons. To survive in this business over the long haul, Kingman advises me, a girl needs to be versatile.

The other great news is that Cliff has been hired to be the show's head cameraman. We plan to commute to the studio together each morning in a chauffeured Lincoln Town Car—just like Kingman's. I'm also pleased to report that Frank has resigned his doorman duties to become our driver, which should leave him more time to pursue his passion for rearranging furniture. My former bodyguards, Abdoul and Waldo, who were unfairly dismissed by their security firm when I bolted from *Filthy Rich!* will be sharing Frank's old shift. To supplement their pay, they've arranged to work part-time at the Gap.

As for my ex, Neil, I read recently in a "Page Six" item

that since getting bawled out by me on *Filthy Rich!* he's moved out to the Hamptons, expanding his adult orthodontic practice to include tooth-whitening services in hopes of attracting celebrity patients. My former client Jane McDee has moved herself and her many bandannas out there, too. I wish them both well. There were some rough patches, but it seems it all turned out for the best. We're even now.

Given a choice, I'd still prefer to be famous for something more uplifting—negotiating a Middle East peace, say, or concocting a diet cola drink that surpasses Diet Coke. Saving an endangered species would be nice. But as I said at the very beginning, life is full of funny twists and turns. Overall, I think I've been pretty lucky.

Finally, here it is: your own revised and updated pocket-size copy of Marcy's Magnificent Seven, my personal rules for a healthy, happy life. Clip it to keep in your wallet or tape to your bathroom mirror. Refer to it often. It helps. Really. Look where it got me.

MARCY'S MAGNIFICENT SEVEN

1. Be bold! But don't take unnecessary risks!
2. Shun fattening foods.
3. Keep your sunny side up.
4. Moisturize.
5. Avoid horizontal stripes.★
6. Big elbows are always in fashion.
7. Remember to floss.★★

★Marcy's original Rule Number Five, "Watching daytime TV is degenerate," has been changed, in keeping with Marcy's brand-new job responsibilities.

★★Marcy has come to believe that there are things more important than remembering to floss.